THE ATOMICS

OTHER BOOKS BY PAUL MAUNDER

Rainbows in the Mud:
Inside the Intoxicating World of Cyclocross

The Wind at my Back:
A Cycling Life

THE ATOMICS

PAUL MAUNDER

Lightning Books

Published in 2021
by Lightning Books Ltd
Imprint of Eye Books Ltd
29A Barrow Street
Much Wenlock
Shropshire
TF13 6EN

www.lightning-books.com

ISBN: 9781785632327

Cover by Nell Wood
Typeset in Sabon LT Std

British Library Cataloguing in Publication Data
A catalogue record for this book is available from the British Library.

Printed by CPI Group (UK) Ltd, Croydon CR0 4YY

For Lesley

PART ONE

1

URANIUM

Oxford, March 1968

Since the trial Frank had been on a leave of absence. *Pending further psychological evaluation*, the letter from the Authority said. So instead of driving the familiar route past wintry fields to the facility at Barton Hall, he went for a walk. Every day, shortly after Gail left for work, he swung on an old waxed jacket, filled his pockets with lemon sherbets, and set out into the sharp spring mornings. Their flat was at one end of a street which, at first glance, may have seemed respectable, lined as it was by Victorian villas and expansive trees whose roots ruptured the paving stones. Look again, however, and there was a mattress dumped in a front garden, a car on bricks, windows boarded up.

On this last day of March the sun sliced low over the chimneys. A soft wind carried the clang of barrels being unloaded at the pub on the corner. Frank thought of his street as representing a border, a transition between the *nice* roads to the north, where academics and wealthy students lived, and the *not-so-nice* roads to the south, crowded by workers from the Cowley car plants. Frank liked to be perverse, walking east along this imaginary borderline, as if reserving his loyalty. He had no allegiances. Not to town, not to gown. His line of work was cold and hard and unforgiving, like a steel blade. He saw the physical world around him – the brick walls, the parked cars, the overgrown front gardens – as bloated. Beneath the surface hummed the true layers of existence: the atoms and molecules too tiny for humans to crush.

This was his truth. His secret universe, invisible to all but a lucky few. Only a handful of men in the world did what Frank did. He was an expert in instability. His days, at least before all this nonsense, were spent bent over a microscope, examining radioactive material for signs of degradation.

And now... Now he just walked.

Past the little parade of shops. A decrepit old woman pushing a shopping trolley, a younger woman staring at her toddler. The mother as pale as a cadaver. Children did that to you. Beyond the shops was a metal gate, giving onto a small park – just a scrap of green hemmed in by ramshackle gardens. On its other side was an alleyway that led to the canal.

A very serious criminal incident...the letter had gone on to say. *We need to ensure that you are wholly fit to return to work and do not pose a threat to yourself, your colleagues or the wider community.* Was this to be another trial? Hadn't the police done their job to everyone's satisfaction? Would he have to become a monkey in the Authority's laboratory just to get back to work? He missed his work. Away from it he was getting weaker, mentally and physically. Yes he'd been found guilty. There were too many witnesses to realistically expect any other outcome. But a suspended sentence meant he should be able to return to work immediately. He was a good man. He'd acted to protect the girl, in her interests.

When the letter came he composed a reply, informing the Authority that the only way they would get inside his head would be to split it open with an axe. Of course, Gail had opened and read the letter before he'd had a chance to post it, immediately ripping it to shreds. *Idiot* was the only word she'd said to him that evening.

As he neared the entrance to the alleyway, Frank noticed a couple on the other side of the grass, following the other path towards it. They were moving very slowly and seemed to be conversing quietly, their heads leaning together, though not in the manner of lovers. The man was dressed in a dark overcoat and had a rather comical shape – all shoulders and chest, teetering on tiny feet in dainty polished shoes. His companion was slight and walked with a stoop. She too had on a dark coat, beneath which a green dress swished around her knees. A black hat was pulled low over her eyes.

The pair separated, the man darting forward so that he reached the entrance to the alleyway ahead of Frank, who hesitated. But on seeing that the woman had stopped to light a cigarette, he carried on. They were having an argument, or perhaps the man was late for an appointment. Now they were between two fences, brambles and blackberry bushes narrowing the gravel path, their crunching footsteps falling into a rhythm. The man was ahead, his upper body swaying. Then Frank. Then the woman, for she followed him into the alleyway.

And just as Frank realised that the three of them were walking at the same speed, and wasn't that a bit strange, the man stopped and turned around. Frank was about to say *excuse me*, but out came a pair of fists like mallets. One hand grabbed Frank's lapel, the other jabbed him hard enough that he tottered backwards and wound up sitting on his backside.

The man's coarse, florid face loomed over him, breathing cigarette fumes as he shoved Frank's shoulders to the ground, then knelt on his ribs. His weight was crushing. The woman in the green dress stooped over them both. Now the smell of cigarettes was overcome with a sickly floral scent. Somewhere above them a crow began to laugh.

Her face was skeletal. White skin stretched over bone. Clownish make-up dragged across her lips and eyes. And those eyes... The fury in them made Frank's body twist in fear. An icy burning sensation tore across his skin and his mind filled with noise as he made the connection. The woman in the magistrates' court who'd shouted from the public gallery. *Justice, this is not justice.*

Her bruising accomplice backed off and she sank onto her haunches, her knees now on Frank's chest, though she was no weight at all. And from her fingers flashed a short blade.

'For my boy,' she said. Her voice was hoarse and carried a country burr.

There was no pain as she pulled the knife across his face, starting at his temple and cutting diagonally, through an eyebrow, skimming his eyelid, deep into his cheek and down to the corner of his mouth, where she finished with a flick.

Heat spread across his skin, blood climbing out of his new fissure. Blackness. Swimming colours and sounds. A kick in the stomach that he barely felt because now came the pain screaming in.

2

REACTOR

When the ward was silent save for some low snoring from the old boy over by the window, when the stale hospital air began to choke him, when the painkillers began to wear off, he heard her footsteps echoing in the corridor. The nurses could not see anyone. They saw only their patient's crazed eyes, not the lunatic who hunted him.

Pinned down by blankets, his face swaddled in gauze and bandages, Frank listened in rigid terror. She was coming for him. The cut had not satisfied her, she wanted to slash him again and again, to rip skin from bone. Some nights the footsteps went on for hours, rising and falling along the corridors, and dawn began to creep around the curtains before he could rest easy. Other nights the sound was fleeting, barely there, and he was able to drift into uneasy sleep.

Once, Frank's eyes cracked open to find her standing over him. He cried out and swiped her arm away. A thermometer smashed on the floor and the nurse who'd been about to administer it jumped clear of his reach.

Other voices came swimming through the light, too.

'We've got her,' said a policeman.

'My poor baby, 'said Gail.

'A pound of flesh,' said his father.

When Gail first visited after his stitch-up session, they sat in silence, holding hands. She had on her beige mac with the big brown buttons, bright blue wool trousers, her hair pinned up. A heavy silence. A tear from his uncovered eye rolled onto the side of his nose and stopped there. Bandages absorbed tears from his wounded eye. Gail cried too, though like everything she did it was intense, demonstrative and quickly forgotten. A blow of the nose and a wave of the hand, and a thin bluster of humour took over.

'What am I going to do with you?' she said.

He said nothing. His lips were swollen, dry and cracked, and it felt like any movement might tear his stitches apart. A dull ache pulsed up and down the line of the cut. It was his eye, taped shut, that hurt the most. The doctors said his sight was never in danger because the knife had cut open his eye-lid and only scratched his eyeball, but he could tell from the look on their faces that they were worried about something.

That was two days ago. Two days in this bed, mummified, at the mercy of others. With that knife she had cut him in two. He was divided now. There would always be a scar to split left from right, past from present.

His life now had two chapters: before her, after her.

Her name was Andrea. Devoted mother, knife-wielder, harpy. A mother of four from Didcot, the boy was her eldest. The police said they knew the family well.

'Lou has asked if I want to go out tomorrow night,' Gail said. Louise, her colleague from school, didn't like Frank. He could tell by the way she looked at him. 'You don't mind do you? I'll come here first for an hour, then get the bus into town. I'd only be sitting at home on my own.'

Though Gail often went out with her girlfriends, and she was right in saying that she'd otherwise be alone at home – visiting hours ended at eight, Frank felt somehow aggrieved. Something grated about her assumption that he wouldn't object. Did she think she held more power over him now?

Yes, he was a prisoner, weakened by being opened up, but he would recover and rebuild. There was work to do.

• • •

In the snug bar of the Lamb and Flag, with a fire crackling in the hearth, honeyed light refracting through pints of beer and a good-natured hum of conversation, Gail felt the relief of escape. She and Lou sat close together on a bench, sipping their gins and looking out into the crowd of drinkers.

'He keeps looking over, that one, yes, that one in the blue scarf,' said Lou, who was, to use a word Gail's mother liked, incorrigible.

'Oh stop it,' said Gail, shaking her head, but with a smile. 'I feel bad enough for coming out.'

It was true though. The man by the bar did keep looking over, and it wasn't Lou his eyes came back to. He was tall and slender, with an intensity in his face that she found attractive. Gail wasn't interested in buffoons. Christ, that was her problem wasn't it? Serious, intense men were exciting but, as she was finding out, unpredictable as hell.

Again, he looked over. Lou giggled and raised her glass to him. He quickly looked away, unable to cope with this level of communication.

Annoyed that her friend was still engaging in such acts of frivolity while Gail's husband lay in the John Radcliffe Hospital, Gail said, 'He'll be scarred for life, they told me. Across his face, I mean.'

'I bet he's wishing he hadn't got off so lightly at court. Wouldn't have happened if he'd gone to prison.'

'Lou…' Gail said, frowning, though the same thought had occurred to her.

'Would have made it easier for you to leave him too. If he'd gone down I mean. Now you'll be playing nursemaid to Frankenstein.'

'I'm not leaving him. He needs me.'

'Gail, you know what he did to that boy. *He* will never be the same again. God, it's a wonder his mother didn't cut his throat rather than just his face. I'm telling you, you need to get out of that marriage. How do you know he won't do it to you one day?'

'I just know. He's not a madman. He thought he was doing the right thing, protecting the girl. Remember that boy gave her a black eye. Frank got carried away, but he thought he was doing it to avenge her. He gets…he gets these ideas in his head, and it's like he's blind to everything else, and sometimes his way of looking at the world is so black and white, particularly when it comes to people, and...well, when it comes to people there are so many shades of grey. I don't know, it's hard to explain. But fundamentally he's not a bad man.'

Lou opened her mouth as if to fire back a response, then closed it. Took a drink and stared off into the room. Gail knew what was going through her head. She was thinking that Gail sounded like every other wife who stood by an abusive husband. And Lou also knew how much Gail wanted a baby. Both women were thirty-two, and Lou had two daughters. She also had a successful and adorable husband, so could only justify infidelity by trying to stir it up for her friends.

When other men paid her attention, as they often did (though God knows why, she felt her youthful energy ebbing away every morning), Gail frequently played through a variation on the same thought process. About how life was essentially a narrowing of options, and a question of timing. She had been a few days shy of her thirtieth birthday when she met Frank and decided he had potential. Like a house standing alone on a hillside, unloved and with a dark past, he'd become her project. She loved his intelligence, his looks, his wry way of looking at the world. He didn't drink and he didn't lust after other women (or at least, if he did, he was very subtle about it). He was different. Though didn't every woman say that about the man they fell for?

So different. Crazed, one witness had said in court. He wanted to beat the life out of that boy – that was plain as could be. If he hadn't been pulled off, who knows? It could have been a murder charge... So many voices and opinions, but there were pieces of testimony that Gail couldn't forget. Every day she'd gone to the magistrates' court and sat hunched in her seat, feeling sick, ashamed of him, hating him for putting her in this position. Nothing she heard was really a surprise, not really. That he was capable of violence. That he had some misguided notion in his brain about looking after that miserable stringy girl who worked with him at the facility and started all this off by getting pregnant by a boy who was engaged to someone far prettier. He'd reacted to the news with a punch to her face, then Frank had decided to retaliate on her behalf. Not that he was in love with the girl – oh no, he was very clear on that (and Gail believed him).

Gail looked at the man in the blue scarf. Perhaps he was married, had children. Had that terrible affliction – the wandering eye. How many options did she have now? Leaving Frank was possible – it was – but not tonight.

• • •

Frank woke with an electric spasm. Confused, unable to establish where he was, he held himself very still and listened. There was the incessant tick of the clock on the wall opposite, someone grumbling in their sleep, a lone car on the ring road below. And closer, much closer, a new sound. Breathing, but not like any of the breathing sounds he'd grown accustomed to over the past two nights. This was a rasping, urgent and intense. And it was coming from the bed next to his, the one always surrounded by screens. He sensed, but could not see, movement. A body twisting under the pressure of sheer terror. Eyes that searched the ceiling in desperation, soon to be closed forever. Feet kicking uselessly, hands scrabbling at a noose that would not give. His mother's body arching unnaturally in its final moments, her consciousness already exploding, her will to live long departed. Soon she would be free from her demons, and from her husband whose cruelty consisted mainly of refusing to acknowledge that she had any demons. And she would never see her son's beautiful face sliced in two.

Frank inhaled sharply and the image, the sounds, vanished. The poor sod in the next bed went on softly snoring. The clock went on ticking.

He'd never tried to commit suicide, but he thought about it often enough. The method, the timing, the impact. Sometimes, standing on a tube platform, his toes began shuffling forward, involuntarily, without any conscious decision being made, and he had to tip his body backwards to force them back from the edge. He could anticipate the moment of breathless hanging in mid-air, the final blast of life before the thwack of the train and the bone-crunching down among the gravel and tracks and rat shit. A tidy way to go, really. The train companies were used to washing people's brains off their advertisements. Some delays, a strong cup of tea for the driver, and everyone would get on with their day again.

But he would never kill himself. It was too weak, too feeble-minded. Just supposing he did, he knew he would surely make a better job of it than his mother had. After the third attempt he'd been so angry with her he told her precisely where she'd gone wrong each time. Not enough pills, learn to tie a decent noose, throw yourself off something higher. I'm indestructible, she smiled. And for a long time it had seemed she was, at least physically. It wasn't long after that Dad moved her into Parkview, a bland name for a place of such anguish.

There she had cleverly managed to asphyxiate herself by tying her dressing gown belt into a noose, securing the other end to the bed frame, then sliding out of bed. Finally, after all those amateurish attempts, she became expert at suicide.

3

CONTAINMENT

Three months later

Bloody thing. Why won't it move?

Cigarette clamped between his lips, one hand on the steering wheel, Frank tugged at the window handle, trying to gauge how hard he could pull before it came off. A quarter-turn then it stopped. He glanced back at the road, wriggled in his seat and tried again with more force. Bloody thing.

A quick acidic reaction coursed through his chest. He banged the wheel with the palm of his hand. The anxiety that had been twisting through him all morning, souring the whole journey, now fused into something stronger, a more satisfying anger.

He looked across at Gail. Fed up with talking to him

she'd put her seat back and gone to sleep even before they'd got clear of Oxford. She was hungover of course. While he'd finished the packing and cleaned the flat, she'd gone out for a 'quick goodbye drink' with her girlfriends, eventually stumbling in at ten to one. By the time she'd managed to haul herself out of bed he had the car packed and everything else sitting in the hallway for the removal men, who, apparently taking their cue from his wife, turned up forty-five minutes late. Drinking cups of tea and chain-smoking, she sat at the kitchen table in her dressing gown while he stripped their bed, picked up her dress from the bedroom floor and supervised the loading of the van. As soon as they left it began to rain.

In the newly-freshened light her skin looked marbled, the daubs of make-up crude and plasticky. Her mouth was agape, strands of blonde hair stuck along her jaw. He followed the collar of her dress down to where her breasts pulled the printed cotton taut, creating little gaps to peer through, then down over the bulge of her tummy. It was one of her favourite dresses – she'd laid it out yesterday afternoon, with matching shoes. The tender white of her thighs was visible where the dress split, wobbling a little when the car bounced over a pothole. Frank put a hand to his crotch. And as he hardened, so, obscurely, did his anger. He drove faster, eyes flicking between the road and his wife's body. Sweat pricked at his temples until a single bead trickled towards the corner of his eye. He needed some air. The bloody car was too hot. Gail gave a little snort and rolled her head away from him. Frank reached down to the window handle and wrenched it so hard it snapped off in his hand.

• • •

The land was broad and low. Featureless, save for the church steeples that pricked the streaked sky at regular intervals. At school he'd been a decent cross-country runner. His favourite event, the biggest of the autumn calendar, was a steeplechase starting and finishing in the Somerset village where he lived, looping out across the Levels to take in three other villages. The memory was still vivid. Splashing and leaping along the edges of waterlogged fields, lungs rasping, fingers numb, looking up for the next bobbing steeple, knowing there would be a crowd in the village to cheer the runners on.

Now he was going to reclaim the sense of space, of a limitless horizon, that he'd possessed at ten years old. Of Setonisle, their new home, he had only a few blurred images in his mind – he'd only visited once before agreeing to the job and hadn't been allowed to take pictures. The man from the Authority had painted it as an incredible opportunity for his career, for his reputation, but he wasn't fooled. They just wanted him away from Barton Hall, away from the scene of the crime. The boy's mother, Andrea, had gone to prison and her friends were deluging the facility chief with threatening letters. So Frank was to be redeployed to the Seton One power station, so far east that it was practically in Finland. No interview, no psychological evaluation (despite what their letter had said), no choice. They just made it happen. The day of his visit, in May, had been unseasonably cold. The wind blasted off the dark North Sea waves and excoriated him as he stood in the middle of a labyrinth of metal and concrete.

Frank lit another cigarette, rolled the car around a lumbering tractor. Over the summit of a low hill he could see fields stretching ahead, a giant jigsaw puzzle. A pair of larks sketched arcs against the cornflower sky. For the first time that morning he felt free of Oxford. He hadn't realised just how much the city bore down on his shoulders. Out here he was able to breathe, to ease the perpetual frown that, he knew, put strangers on edge. Looking across at Gail he felt a sudden nagging sense of gratitude that she would follow him out here, that she would give up her own job, her friends, her nights out in the West End. Their new life would be very different.

'Where are we?' she said, twisting forward in her seat and squinting against the sunshine.

'Not sure really,' he lied brightly, for he knew they were on the A14, 77 miles from their destination. 'Somewhere in deepest darkest Suffolk.'

'What happened to the rain?'

'It stopped.'

'More scientific magic, huh?'

She had once asked him what electricity is. After he explained the basics, clearly and concisely, she'd repeated the question. Yes, but *what* is it? I can't see it, I can't touch it, I can't smell or taste it. So how do I know it exists?

Gail lived a sensual life. For her, the world was immediate and raw. She reacted to what she could see in front of her and ignored the abstract, the ethereal. It wasn't that she was stupid; just that all her intelligence flowed through her emotions. Other people's problems weighed on her, and other people's joy buzzed through her. In company, her sensitivity to others made Frank ashamed of his own coldness. If he ever said as much to her, she told him he needed his detachedness, it was part of him, part of what enabled his work. He had no explanation for what attracted her to him other than that hackneyed maxim; opposites attract.

She turned to gaze out over the land. Originally a Londoner, she saw only blankness when she looked at a place like this.

'Beautiful,' she said. 'A fresh start eh? An adventure.'

He nodded and turned to look at her. She smiled tenderly but her eyes crept to the scar on his face, following it down from his forehead to his mouth. Over the last months, since it happened, he'd grown used to this silent communication. Her eyes travelling along the wide pink mark like a plastic stripe melted into his face. It was, he supposed, quite something to get used to, this disfigurement of one's husband. As far as possible he avoided mirrors, but he couldn't help the unconscious movement of his index finger to his face. Sometimes he caught himself stroking the scar. It was a mark of silence between them. The screaming, the doors slamming, had all happened while the dressings were clinging to his ridiculous face. When the dressings came off the scar began to harden, and so did their tacit agreement not to speak of what he'd done to deserve it.

Gail arched her back, stretched her arms forward and yawned loudly.

'I'm famished, what are we doing for lunch?'

They found a village big enough to have a string of whitewashed shops, parked the car and levered out their stiffened limbs. A blessed relief to be out in the fresh air. Having climbed into the car in rainy Oxford, then gradually filled it with cigarette smoke, it was something of a shock to be standing in the middle of this village street, sunlight bouncing along the cottages, a breeze carrying the scent of roses past them, and a workman's van put-putting in the distance, no more urgent than the plump bumble bee that came to land on Frank's shoulder.

'Oh hello little one,' exclaimed Gail.

With a grimace, Frank shook the welcome party off his jacket and set off towards a bakery.

•••

There was an idea in Gail's mind of a life lived in a place like this. Among the genteel and the ignorant, with walks in the countryside and coffee mornings, a tiny village school, harvest festival and all that traditional bumpkin stuff. She'd grown up in a similar place in Wiltshire, a village nestled underneath the Downs, and though her parents had uprooted them all to south London when she was eight, those early memories remained.

She felt terrible. It had been a heavy night. How many pubs had they waltzed in and out of? Oh, and Lou falling slap into the gutter, and Candia trying to kiss that policeman... She was going to miss her friends.

Twice, no, three times she had decided not to go. To the lounge bar of The Bear she announced, fuck it, I'm not going. And everyone cheered her tremendous bravery. Ten minutes later she was crying and telling some total stranger how much her husband needed her. In the Turf Tavern she called out, it's over – I'm getting a divorce, and was rewarded with a spontaneous round of applause. A giddy, anything-seems-possible moment. But once outside the rain sobered her up just enough to crack her courage. In the end someone, a man with a scar on his face (though nowhere near as long as Frank's), listened to her story and made the not unreasonable suggestion that she go (after all, it *was* a little late to pull out), and see how she felt in a month's time. If she was unhappy she could always leave her husband then. As he spoke his hand moved up her leg.

So here she was, her head being pummelled by this gruesome sunshine, in desperate need of bread and water and sugar. And there, outside the bakery Frank was striding towards, was just the sight she didn't wish to see. Of course Frank didn't notice, just breezed past. But Gail's eyes were drawn, helplessly, to the young woman and her pram. She looked so happy, with rosy cheeks as clichéd as the village she apparently lived in, and the baby (impossible not to look into a pram, and always the parents *wanted* you to) was a fat doughy bundle underneath a knitted red blanket. The young mother looked at Gail, expecting kind words, but received only a grudging smile.

• • •

Reluctant to get back in the car so soon, they carried the paper bag of cheese rolls and bottles of lemonade to a churchyard down the street. Framing its dilapidated wooden gates was a brick arch, itself almost lost in the greenery of a monstrous black poplar. As Frank passed underneath the arch he noticed a slab of stone topping it with an inscription worn to obscure hieroglyphics.

'Come on,' she said, as he hesitated. 'There's no rush to get there is there?'

'We've got to meet the removal men.'

'They'll wait. Anyway, won't they stop for their own lunch?'

Gail took his hand and led him towards the church. On both sides of the path gravestones stood crooked as old men's teeth. The lush grass around them was wild with daisies and dandelions. They found a bench and sat in silence, pulling at the soft white rolls. Crumbs lay scattered in her lap until she stretched out her legs, shut her eyes and pulled her dress up over her knees. The sunshine glowed iridescent on her skin. Lemonade glistened on her lips.

Unable to get comfortable on the bench, Gail moved to the grass by his feet. Wiggled into a comfortable furrow, hands knitted underneath her head, legs crossed at the ankles. Frank watched the rise and fall of her belly. How slim and delicate life was. How contingent.

'Come down here,' she said. He clambered down onto his knees, then slumped beside his wife. Her hand found his arm and spidered along it.

'Some day,' she murmured, 'we'll be lying like this, only six feet down.'

'Not me, I'm not going to be compost. Cremation. That's the way to go.'

She heaved herself up onto an elbow and, blinking sweat and dust from her eyes, looked across at him. There was reproach in her eyes. Christ, this was one of her things; the belief that love was total and eternal, that not being buried together was some kind of betrayal.

'I thought we'd agreed we'd be buried together under an oak tree? Or has that changed now?'

There was that word again. Now. Now. Now. Like a bird

pecking at his temple. The implication that recent events had altered everything. That any previous contracts were null and void. He'd been attacked, because he'd stood up for a defenceless girl, a girl carrying a baby, and yet somehow this fact had been twisted. Not for the first time he wondered whether Gail wanted to leave him, but had been too cowardly. His body stiffened, his head buzzed. But he knew he had to push down this anger.

'Let's not talk about it. It's a long way off. We'll change our minds a dozen times before then.'

'I won't,' she said.

She nuzzled her nose into his throat, inhaled long, swung one of her legs on top of his. As she lifted her face to his and their lips touched he tasted lemonade, salt, tobacco. Her tongue came flicking, digging into his mouth. His fingers slipped into the warmth of her hair.

'I don't know why you stick it out,' he said.

'Because I love you,' she replied, a little too quickly. 'And I think we can be happy out here. You, me, baby.'

That's it. That's what you want. The seed in your tummy. And then what? Will you stay, or will you leave?

'I'm a good man, Gail. I want a quiet life. Do my work, have a family, look after you all. Nothing more than that.'

'You don't need to tell me. I know that. I understand you.'

Sometimes he used to lie awake at night, with Gail asleep beside him, thinking of Karen, of that boy hitting her. And the thought of it made him so angry that he had to go into the living room, drink some Scotch, fold himself into a ball of primal anger on the carpet. God, if Gail had ever woken and discovered him like that. Why? Why had the sight of that bruised face made him react so vehemently?

The ragged cry of a rook. He looked up, panicked, expecting to see a black shape diving at him. No, only blue sky and the swaying branches of an elm tree, sunlight glowing through its leaves. Turning his head he could see a row of houses with high shining windows. And behind every one...something was watching. Invisible, cloaked in darkness, but a strong presence nonetheless. All its focus was on him. He felt its gaze trying to claw into him, to prise something from the depths of him, something ancient and guttural.

He pushed Gail until she buckled sideways and fell into the grass.

'Not here, Christ,' he muttered.

She sat up and began adjusting her clothes. 'What's the matter, not part of the schedule?'

Frank got to his feet. His mind felt like it was burning, swarming. The churchyard roared. He didn't dare look up at the windows. Gail was talking at him, glaring, shaking her head, but he was already walking away, tripping over gravestones. In the earth the dead were laughing at him. Live now, they were crying, give in to your anger!

He was afraid of himself and had to keep walking, leaving Gail to her confused tears. This place was crumbling and redundant. Like going back in time. Christ, the world was going to move on. The future would be bright and clean and men like him, scientists, the rational minds, would be heroes. No dirt, no mess, no emotion.

Where he was going he would create such power. Clean, effective and devastating. He'd seen the pictures of Nagasaki. Imagine an atomic bomb landing here in this village. A flash of light and all of this turned to ash.

The ancient church blown away on the wind, as if God had lost his patience and exhaled too sharply. The future, the future.

• • •

If she was quick to temper, Gail was just as quick to forgive. She flared, then fizzled out. No long-burn glowering. It was one of the things he appreciated about her. Within an hour, without many words being exchanged, they were at ease with each other again. She would, he knew, be disappointed in his lack of spontaneity and daring, but she could hardly be surprised. And for his part he regretted flouncing out of the churchyard like that. She'd once called him melodramatic, and how he'd burned with the truth of her assessment.

He was ashamed too of his self-contradiction. How can you rant about science and rational thought when you're scared of rooks and dark windows?

The road rolled away under the wheels of the car, and the landscape went on; seemingly infinite, ever-changing, repetitive. Hedgerows and fields of wheat, tracks leading away to woods, whispers of cloud on the horizon.

The petrol gauge needle flickered closer to Empty. In a village he found a petrol station and brought the car to a halt on the forecourt. No one appeared from the brick shed, so Frank unhooked the pump and filled the car up himself.

Inside the shed it was so dim it took his eyes a moment to adjust. The air was cool and hung with dust. Judging by the few bowing shelves on the back wall, with piles of chocolate bars and tins of condensed milk, the owner was making a half-hearted attempt at the retail trade. The rest of the room was filled with sacks of something agricultural. Frank picked his way across the concrete floor to a table, behind which sat a young girl. There was a battered money-box in front of her which he guessed amounted to a till.

'Suddenly I feel a long way from town,' he said cheerfully.

The girl looked at him as if he had just landed from outer space. As he looked at her he realised she was older than he'd initially thought, perhaps in her early twenties. Sullen but not bad-looking. In the gloom her eyes were the brightest lights.

'A pound exactly,' he said, offering her a five-pound note. With an almost imperceptible sigh, she got up from her chair, edged around the table and came towards him. A sudden rush of adrenaline inflamed him. Her dark hair, cut short, was greasy and tucked behind her ears, the small white undulations at the base of her throat glowed pearly white. She was nearly as tall as him, and slender at the waist. When she stepped past him he caught her scent.

Through the small filthy window he watched her cross the forecourt and study the petrol pump's gauge. Did he also see her peer into the car at Gail ?

'One pound,' she said when she came back, as if she'd gone to a great deal of trouble and calculation to come to the figure. Holding the fiver out, he took a step towards where she stood and her eyes widened. Her eyes couldn't resist his, but it was fear they showed, not attraction. No, he wanted to say, you don't have to be scared of me. I'll protect you. That's what I do. She tried to take a step back but butted up against the table, scrabbled his change from the money-box and held out four pound notes.

'Take it,' she said.

Take her, another voice whispered. *Grab her*.

As he tried to untangle these two voices – one real, one in his head – his fingers curled into fists. Frozen, all breath suspended, the girl's eyes raged against him. I don't want to hurt you, he wanted to say.

She thought that he desired her, but he did not. He wanted her to know what he was capable of. That he understood men and their base urges, that if asked he would protect her just as he had protected Karen. It was hard to convey this, even in words, but the girl's eyes were firmer now. She understood. As he uncurled his fingers her breathing steadied.

Light-footed and happy, he walked back to the car, slid in and started the engine. Smiling at his wife, he said, 'Not far to go now darling.'

4

NEUTRON

As he drove on towards the coast, he realised that, strangely, the only person who understood him was Andrea. He'd seen it in her eyes as she bent over him with the knife. Revenge, yes, but also connection. And later, in the hospital, once he'd eliminated the fear of her, Frank had felt neutral about her presence in the corridors, even wished for it. Her violence and his were intermingled, as were their motives. He'd been sticking up for that stringy girl, Karen (who reminded him of a girl he'd loved when he was twelve years old), and Andrea was sticking up for her debased son. On his last night in hospital, in the pre-dawn haze between waking and dreaming, he had felt her fingers slip into his. Thin and cold yet comforting. When he looked around he could not see her. But he could taste her flowery perfume hanging over his face like a net.

In the blink of an eye, he saw it. Stamped on the brake and threw the car into reverse. The hedgerow rewound until he came to the five-bar gate, where he jumped out to get a better look.

So beautiful.

So simple. And such a statement. The main reactor building was a huge gleaming white box. No markings, no fuss and no clues as to what lay inside. Standing proud on the shoreline, it was surrounded by smaller conventional buildings, some still under construction. Beyond it, looking north-east, the sea shimmered. A fishing boat emerged from behind the reactor.

'That's it,' he said to Gail, who had joined him, their elbows lined up along the warm metal gate. 'Incredible isn't it?'

She didn't reply immediately, which was unlike her. He sensed her disquiet.

'It's totally safe. Cleaner than a coal-mine or a gasworks. It's the future for energy in this country.' Christ, he sounded like a promotional leaflet. She didn't care about any of that.

A mile along the coast was the jumble of rooftops of Setonisle, the small fishing village that was to be their new home. Before the power station it had been an anonymous little place, one of a string of villages along this gently curving coastline, separated by sandy beaches and low, crumbling cliffs. Inland, beyond the salt-marshes, the land was good for crops and orchards. Offshore the miserable bulk of the North Sea crouched, ready to whip up a storm at any moment.

• • •

On that cold May day, after a tour of the reactor site, the Director of Chemistry, a man called Parker, had driven Frank to a harbour-side pub for a warming glass of whisky and a meat pie. In the power station their conversation had been stiff, but there was always the common ground of work. They could talk about the operation, Frank's new job, the problems they'd been encountering with reactor fuel. Away from the site, unable to talk in public about the power station for fear of being overheard, they were faced with the terror of small-talk.

Parker's eyes returned again and again to Frank's scar. The last dressing had been removed a week before and Frank was still getting used to his new appearance. All the time he'd had the dressings, as ridiculous as he looked, it had seemed there was a chance that when they were removed he would look just as he did before the attack. No scar, no marks, history erased. Wishful thinking, of course. He was now a monster who frightened little children. The scar was mottled pink and red. In certain lights it shone like thick oil paint. When he went out he could see people tracing its path across his face – their eyes always travelled from top to bottom, as her knife had.

How much did Parker know? Well, as much as the Authority would tell him. Enough. Frank was a problem being moved on. Parker was being screwed. And yet he said nothing about it.

To revive their conversation Frank discreetly enquired why the village was suffixed with isle, when it patently stood on the mainland. 'Good question,' Parker replied, 'and one I happen to have an answer for. The story goes that there used to be a village atop an island, thirty miles out to sea. Hundreds of years ago, mind.'

At this point Parker inserted a theatrical pause and gazed out of the window at the grey sea beyond the harbour wall.

'But the Lord of this island,' he continued, 'was cruel. Lord Seton was his name. He had three sons; loved the eldest, tolerated the middle son and hated the youngest. Made his life hellish. Eventually the youngest boy could stand it no longer and with the help of a warlock he summoned the sea to punish his father. He chained his father to the gates of the castle and while the villagers fled to the mainland the Lord was drowned. The eldest son, however, survived, and by all accounts wasn't half as bad as his father, so when the villagers rebuilt the village they kept the name. The deference of the English peasant eh?'

'And the island?' Frank asked.

'Still out there beneath the waves,' said Parker. 'But...' and now he lowered his voice in mock conspiracy '... legend has it that a month after the great flood some fishermen went out there to look for a stash of gold reputed to be hidden in the castle, and when they dived down to the gate, what did they see? Nothing. Lord Seton's chains were unbroken but he had gone. No skeleton, not a sign of him.'

'Perhaps he became a nuclear physicist,' Frank said, and got a laugh.

Parker went on: 'They say he haunts this coast still, hunting for his treasonous son.'

• • •

Gail gazed out at the silver-blue blur of land, beach, sea. She said, 'Imagine living in such a quiet little place and having this thing land on you. You know we might not be terribly popular among the locals.'

'Oh come on, we're bringing jobs, money, people. New life. In a couple of years this place will be twice the size. New children at the school, plenty of work for the local builders, plenty of thirsty scientists in the pubs.'

Again she didn't reply. Idiot, why mention children? Was that where her thoughts had tiptoed off to? He gave her a gentle nudge.

'Let's go and find this chap with the house keys.'

'I need a cup of tea,' she said as they got back into the hot car. 'And a piece of cake.'

'You must have hollow legs,' Frank said, and pulled away.

In a stifling office above a newsagent's, a dour solicitor handed over the keys and gave Frank directions. He needn't have bothered; Frank had already memorised the layout of the village and worked out the location of their new house. He listened politely anyway.

Such was the scale of the workforce required to run Seton One (the authorities had decided to drop the silly island reference) that two hundred new homes were being built in phases over a five-year period. After laughing off the Lord Seton story, Parker proudly told Frank that he'd persuaded the Authority to build the new homes close to the power plant. A statement of confidence, he said, in the safety of this new energy.

Frank drove down to the harbour, pointed out the pub, the fishing boats and the lifeboat station. Gail nodded, squinting her eyes against the sun. He had no idea what she was thinking.

The lane ran north, beside the beach for a while before curving inland behind a rank of sand dunes. To their left were the marshy fields that would soon be a building site for all those new houses. The reactor building hovered in front of them, bizarre and uncompromising. Steam was issuing from two chimneys on the roof of an adjacent shed.

'This must be it,' he said. Ahead, to their left, sat a cluster of bungalows. Cream walls and blush pink roofs, windows sparkling in the sun. As Frank slowed the car he saw the sign declaring Salter Road.

'Oh. A bungalow?' said Gail, in a faux naïve voice that conveyed to him precisely how much she hated the idea of living in a newly built bungalow.

'I told you they were bungalows, I told you that. Let's just get in and get the kettle on, see what's what.'

Along tarmac so new it was still ink-black, they passed a dozen identical bungalows. A few had cars on their drive-ways, all had a front garden of unrolled turf not yet bedded into the ground. How long since the lorry had come round to unload that? Two children were riding bicycles in circles in the centre of a crossroads and gave Frank baleful looks from the pavement once they'd moved aside. Left into Fisher Close. More identical bungalows. More unrolled turf, uniform fences in creosote orange, a shiny dustbin outside each property ready to accept the waste of human lives.

Frank felt sharpened by the strangeness of this place. The newness. The future was here; he could leave behind all that decay and history. As he stepped from the car it was the wind that shocked him. Though the air was warmer than that day in May, the wind gave it a tough edge.

There was a small drift of post behind the front door. Frank stepped over it, wandered into the house, then remembered Gail and turned around.

'Don't I need to carry you over the threshold or something?' he said.

'Save your back,' she said. 'What's it like?'

Frank pretended to care as they trod little pathways into the pristine blue carpet. All he could think about was the power station. He would be comfortable there, happy. The work would keep him busy. He made suitable noises about curtains and the placement of furniture. Not that Gail was particularly interested in home furnishings either. Their flat in Oxford had been a creaking, draughty mess that they never quite found the energy to sort out. Occasionally Gail would disappear to the shops and come back with some extravagant purchases and a determined expression, and there would be a flurry of activity with such disproportionately modest results that her disappointment was palpable. It was a rough old flat; there was no changing that. Her mother said they were still living like students. The old cow.

The kitchen, at the back of the house, had a frosted glass door that opened into the garden. Having always lived in flats, to have a garden at all was something of a novelty. Gail smiled as they stood looking out at the rectangle of grass and three sections of fence. There were no trees or shrubs or flowers.

'Makes me feel like a grown-up,' she said, digging her elbow affectionately into his ribs.

'That's depressing,' Frank said. 'It's hardly a garden at all. On the farm we had these apple trees that were perfect for climbing, and little places you could hide from your parents, places to build a den. That was a garden. Not this. And look – that fence is wonky.'

She turned to look at him, and he knew without returning her gaze what her expression would be.

'Bloody hell Frank, we're here for you. We're here in the middle of nowhere for you. To make a fresh start. I've come with you, haven't I? Sort yourself out.'

At moments like this Frank often found that his brain, capable of resolving the most complex scientific problems, went into protest mode. Shut down, refused to help him by supplying the right words in the right order. With an exasperated sigh, Gail disappeared into their peculiar new home. The removal men arrived ten minutes later, threw their belongings into the front garden and disappeared.

5

ATOM

Tired from the journey, they maintained the low-level bickering as they trudged in and out of the front door, allocating boxes to different rooms. Coming to the front door to collect the last box, Frank found Gail in earnest conversation with a small child. The girl was perhaps four, or five, or maybe older – Frank found children an utter mystery. Dressed entirely in pink, she was clutching a posy of flowers and listening to Gail with a suspicious look in her eyes.

'And this is Frank,' Gail said, and then leaning forward, whispered, 'He's not nearly as grumpy as he looks. Sometimes he can even be quite silly. Frank, this is Lucy. She's four and a half and she lives over the road in number six. She's a little annoyed because she was hoping to have this house for her dollies. She's got twelve dollies and one of them is having a baby, so that will make thirteen.'

'The flowers, Lucy! The flowers! Oh my gosh, I am so sorry.' In a high and penetrating voice a middle-aged woman was calling to them as she marched across the road. She was short, squat and busty, though her brightly patterned and voluminous dress made it hard to accurately assess her figure. Her hair was bundled on top of her head and she looked hot and bothered.

'Hello, hello, I'm Judy. Number six, just over there. This one belongs to me. The advance party, aren't you sweetheart? Now you must never run over the road without Mummy or Daddy. Hello, welcome to our little world. Frank, isn't it?'

Judy thrust out a pink hand for him to shake. Frank forced a smile and saw in Judy's eyes that for all her breeziness and primary colours, she was sharp. As she chimed his name and pumped his hand, her eyebrows raised a fraction. He felt just a little unmasked.

Over her shoulder he saw a man striding up the driveway. Bald save for two grey streaks at the sides of his head, and powerfully built through the chest and shoulders, he wore a faded orange short-sleeved shirt that flared out in the wind, showing flashes of white middle-aged paunch. Incongruously, his trousers were dark and well-tailored. He too thrust a hand at Frank, but his eyes were on Gail.

'Maynard,' he said, in a brusque masculine way. Frank had met plenty of men like this before. He never liked any of them.

'The hubby,' Judy added needlessly.

They did another round of introductions and

handshakes, and Judy listed their children and their children's ages, all of which information Frank made no effort to absorb. Maynard was an engineering manager and had been working at the plant for nine months, overseeing the commissioning of the reactor and the connected electrical systems. It had been quite a journey, he could tell them, quite a journey, and some pretty big scares along the way and…

'Darling, that's enough shop-talk. Plenty of time for all that when you boys go to work in the morning. Why don't you go in together? Maynard can show you around. How to get a cup of tea, that sort of thing. It all sounds like an absolute shambles if you ask me, they can build a nuclear bomb but not organise a canteen to keep the sausage rolls hot.'

'Judy,' said Maynard, with a note of admonition. He obviously took his work far too seriously.

'Sorry, no bomb. Ignore me.' Judy rolled her eyes at Gail, who smiled in sisterly sympathy.

'That is quite a scar you have there,' said Judy, fixing an interrogative gaze up at Frank.

'Judy, Jesus…' Maynard's tone had a crueller edge now.

'That's all right,' said Frank, and as he let his well-rehearsed lie slide out, he felt no guilt, only a delicious sense of complicity with Gail. She would never contradict him in public and he liked that. 'Car crash, with a bus, in Norwich.'

The specificity of this detail made it believable, so the police had said to him. Judy nodded but her eyes traced the line of the scar and he saw a tiny flicker of a frown pass across her brow. She said nothing more and the four of them fell into a brief awkward silence.

'Must have been horrific,' said Maynard.

'So where have you moved from?' asked Gail, directing her question at Judy.

'From leafy Carshalton, Surrey. I must say at first it was like being tipped off the edge of the earth but now we are all settling into it rather well. I mean, when the weather's like this and there's the beach for the children, fresh fish off the boats...' There she seemed to run out of positives and instead gestured vaguely in the direction of the plant as if to say that it was all immaterial anyway. They were Atomics, they followed the work.

'It looks like a lovely village,' Gail said. Not that Maynard was listening; he was much more absorbed in Gail's body. Frank followed Maynard's gaze. The cold sea breeze had hardened her nipples under her thin cotton dress. Frank suppressed his anger. Surely this was an easy crime to forgive among men? Even a cause for husbandly pride. Frank looked quickly back at Judy, who'd been talking and was apparently oblivious to where the attention of the two men was being directed.

'Oh you are going to love it here,' Judy said, the volume of her voice rising as she regained her momentum. 'Honestly, we have so many amazing friends, and we all get on so well. It is such a lovely community already; the kids are in and out of each other's houses. We look after each other, you know?'

'Mummy?'

Maynard winked at Frank. 'Keep away from the locals though. They've got webbed feet and a funny look in their eyes, if you know what I mean.'

'Oh hush Maynard, don't be so horribly superior. Yes, you are brilliant. No, that does not mean you can put everyone else down.'

'Mummy?'

'Well, we will leave you to your unpacking. You must come over when you need a cup of tea and a biscuit. Feel free, anytime. We are an open house for friends and neighbours, absolutely open.'

'Mummy?'

'Yes poppet?'

Lucy was curled around her mother's leg and had been watching Frank, transfixed by his face. Every time he caught her eye, despite his best child-friendly smile, she looked away. Now she looked on the verge of tears. 'My babies were going to live in this house, and *you* said they could. But now these funny-looking people are inside.'

Gail squatted down in front of the girl and engaged her with a winning smile. 'Lucy, I'm sorry that we're moving in. Whenever you want to bring your babies over to our house you're more than welcome. You only have to knock.'

Lucy took a moment to digest this, then melted into a coy smile.

'I'll pick you up in the morning,' Maynard said to Frank, and gave him a firm slap on the shoulder. 'Eight o'clock all right? Good, see you then.'

'Not if I see you first,' Frank replied, deadpan.

Maynard stared back, his eyes bloodshot and mean. Frank sensed a crackle of violence between them, and though he kept his fists balled tight in his pockets he had a startling sensation; that of the warm sprays of blood on his forehead, coming from the boy's nose as he struck it again and again. Maynard's eyes widened a fraction as he took in this stranger's dislike of him.

Then turning away, laughing, he called, 'Good man, good man.'

• • •

In a back corner of their garden was a gate leading into open meadowland, furred with marsh grasses, dotted with tiny flowers. Starlings wheeled and sang. A thin path ran along the back of the houses, dodging various heaps of soil and gravel abandoned by the builders. After a while the path curved away from the houses and ran due east towards the sea. The late afternoon light made incisions into Frank's head. The bristling heat of the day had gone, replaced by a suffusing warmth that seemed to come from the earth rather than blazing down from the sun.

From this perspective Seton One looked benign, even playful, like a piece of modern art that no one could understand. It was silent but, Frank knew, once up close to the reactor a constant hum would be audible. The sound of a million harmoniously moving parts.

They walked in contented silence over the baked earth. The visit from Judy and Maynard had startled them into good humour. Inside the house – their unfamiliar new house – they'd giggled and rolled their eyes. Frank had an unlikely talent for mimicry and Judy was an obvious target.

'Yes, you're brilliant. No that doesn't mean you can put everyone else down,' he said in falsetto.

'My God, she was so over the top. I wonder if she's always like that or whether she was just nervous or something.'

He pulled a face. 'Imagine when she's drunk.'

'And he was just so...boyish. Like a nineteen-year-old lad.'

'I bet he tells me all his stories of derring-do tomorrow. I bet he's got a lot.'

'Please tell me he's not your boss?'

'Doubt it. Different area of the operation. We're about the same level I think.'

'Just don't let him drag you into anything you don't want to do. I know men like him. He'll have you in the pub, shitfaced before you know it.'

His hand nestled in the small of Gail's back as they approached the coast road. Out of habit they stopped and looked both ways before crossing. There was not a single vehicle in sight.

The sand dunes were otherworldly, enchanting. They trudged up, bowled down. White as snow, the sand defied and deceived their footsteps. Ancient fence posts and driftwood planks lay half-submerged.

On the beach they took off their shoes and socks, walked to the water's edge, then turned their backs on the nuclear plant and set off for the village. Every now and then Gail would stoop to pick up a pretty shell or pebble. With the occasional craw of a seagull overhead, the salt-tang of the sea in his nostrils, and wet sand under his toes, Frank could focus on only one thing: fish and chips.

• • •

They sat on the harbour wall with the sun on their necks and the greasy newspaper flower between them. The tide was in. A dozen fishing boats bumped and rattled against each other, water sluicing between them. A few old boys were sitting on a bench outside The Admiral, waiting for opening time. Though the sky overhead was pure blue, out to sea there were daubs of grey and white.

As the vinegar fizzed on his tongue, Frank found himself feeling a strange kind of remorse. Clearly there were specific things he knew he should indeed feel remorse for, yet this feeling now was more oblique. Why, when the world was so beautiful, and there are good people like Gail who will stand by you, why let everyone down? It would be difficult to put his feelings into words, but he knew he must try.

'I'm sorry,' he said quietly. 'That, that I'm not a better person. For you, I mean. I'm sorry you've had to put up with me. I don't deserve you.'

'Don't be silly. You're a good person. You are.' She took his hand, and her touch only intensified his despair. Why hadn't he just left her, come here alone? It would have been better for her, in the long run. She seemed to sense what he was thinking.

'We'll be happy out here,' she said. 'I know we will. Come on, it's a new start isn't it? Away from…everything. All new. I believe in you, I know how special you are. You'll be strong here, I can feel it.'

'You'd be happier without me,' he said.

'But who would buy my chips? I need you for the chips.'

• • •

Tipsy from a couple of pints of the local ale, they walked back along the beach and by the time they got to the sand dunes the midsummer sun was molten orange on the horizon. Turning inland, into the gloaming, Frank pulled Gail, giggling, up the dunes and together they tumbled down the other side, landing in a heap at the bottom. In the meadow they tried and failed to find the path they'd taken before, instead crunching straight through the grass, and Frank walked behind her so that he could take darting looks at the wondrous building away to his right. He wanted to get in there now, into the reactor to get his hands on the fuel rods. He'd have to wait.

Compared to their draughty old flat in Oxford, their new house was stuffy and hot. The windows were locked and neither of them could remember where the keys were. They climbed into bed in their underwear, with only a cotton sheet over them, but while Gail was asleep within moments, lying on her back and snoring, Frank lay awake and stared into the darkness. He hadn't been prepared for just how unsettling this new home would be; not only was the air still and the temperature too warm, but the sounds were different. No longer could he let the gentle rhythm of Oxford send him to sleep. Here there were no buses lumbering between stops, no trains bouncing unseen through the suburbs, no drunk lovers staggering home. There was some noise – a kind of indeterminate moaning that he couldn't quite define. Was it the refrigerator? The wind? Or the power plant?

What would it be like to be hermetically sealed? No fresh air, no way of escape, and every sound muffled. Frank was, he thought, claustrophobic. Those early years in Somerset had imbued him with a sense of wider horizons and outdoor space. Training for a race, he'd run up a nearby hill and stand on its bald summit, recovering his breath and gazing west towards Devon. In that direction lay adventure, perhaps even romance. In his teenage years he had ambitions to travel, to find a way of living that broke out of the plodding routine that – so he thought – consumed his parents' lives. His mother was the romantic, the adventurer, though her travels were mostly in her head. Always a great reader, she would lie with him early in the morning in his little wooden bed, sharing her warmth, describing some far-flung land and its people. Her stories – though they seemed more natural than the 'stories' he found in books – connected wild landscapes, history, folk tales and much more. She had no respect for the line between facts and fiction; to her it was utterly porous. Often she talked about her younger self as the heroine of these travels. He kept his counsel when later he realised she'd never even crossed the English Channel.

The plodding routine served a purpose, Frank was to learn, and any disruptions to it, no matter how apparently inconsequential, could have devastating effects. His immersion, during his early teenage years, into science was a kind of rebellion. It was so totally alien to both his father's farming world and his mother's literary dreaming. Frank loved his mother but he hated the way she let herself be controlled by his father; her weakness. And her distance – when she had one of her spells (which seemed to become more frequent as he got older and spent more time out of the house), she was unreachable, locked inside her suffering.

'Don't bother,' his father had muttered once, coming out of her room to find Frank sitting cross-legged on the landing outside. 'She's gone.'

It was a convenient narrative for his father to weave – the strange son who won't work on the farm, ignores his poor mother and condemns her to troughs of darkness. So much guilt was laid at Frank's feet, like the carcass of a dead animal, parcelled up in greasy paper and left outside the back door.

Often, in the slowest hours of the night, Frank thought of his father lying alone in bed in the farmhouse where Frank had grown up – that cold and unwelcoming place so smothered in ivy that it seemed the natural world wanted to pull the place down – and he could hear his father's thoughts. A constant bilious monologue, spewing out and poisoning the land around the isolated house, killing anything good that wanted to grow. The old bastard's most fiery hate was reserved for Frank's mother. She turned my boy against me, Frank imagined his father thinking, sent him to university, saw that he was out of my reach, then topped herself. Selfish bitch.

Frank's father had a diseased heart. The doctor said it was common in old age, but Frank knew that particular muscle had been black for decades.

He thought of the graveyard. Gail on top of him. The sunlight catching her hair as it hung down. The woman in the green dress – Andrea – in prison somewhere, cursing him. Then the beach. Shells abrasive on the soles of his feet, seaweed drying like parchment, the overlapping licks of the waves. He thought of the village, their new home. And the reactor core, waiting for him.

He dreamt of a wooden shed with a low ceiling, barely any light, piled high with sacks of animal feed, the air choked with a dust that coated his skin as he picked a way through, trying to find the girl with short dark hair. She was crying out words that were unintelligible to him, but he understood the alarm in her voice. Was she trapped?

Where was she? He stumbled and fell to his knees. The dust gathered around his ankles, sucking him down.

He woke disoriented and parched. Gulping down water from the glass beside the bed, he blinked himself awake and swung his legs to the floor. Christ, his head was pounding. Drink some more water, cool down. Wake up enough that the dream won't come back. Breathe, breathe.

From outside came the most unearthly sound. A screaming growl, followed by a high squeal and another desperate growl. Frank went to the window, put his head round the curtain. It was a black night. The sliver of moon offered scant light. In the distance the power station sparkled like a flattened Christmas tree. But the sounds were much closer. He peered into his garden and saw two black shapes writhing together on the grass. A flash of teeth and eyes, a white streak. Badgers fighting. So quick and strong. And the ferocity. He watched, enthralled, the guttural sounds going through him, fizzing down to his fingertips.

6

NUCLEUS

What better way to start the day? Hot toast smeared to the crusts with butter then daubed with Marmite. The salty tang of that weird black stuff against the creaminess. A cup of milky tea to wash it all down. Frank sat alone at the kitchen table, watching the blank wall in front of him. Gail was still in bed.

With the badger interruption, the beer and the heat, he'd slept badly and consequently had a dull throbbing ache at his left temple, but a scalding shower and breakfast would see him ready for the day. He sat upright, his polished black shoes tapping on the vinyl floor. Already the heat was trembling against the windows of the little house.

Maynard had a big blue Rover, which he drove fast and recklessly. Or so it seemed to Frank, who hated being a car passenger. Why they were driving at all was a mystery to him, the plant being less than a mile away, but Frank didn't question the other man. Perhaps arriving on foot wasn't quite the done thing, or perhaps Maynard just wanted to show off his motor. As they pulled away he seemed subdued, less chatty than Frank had expected.

'Bloody children,' Maynard grunted while they waited to turn onto the coast road. Not entirely sure what he meant by this, Frank issued a reciprocal grunt of general empathy. The road was surprisingly busy and there were as many cyclists as cars, all heading in the same direction as them. A pair of girls on old-fashioned bicycles, skirts flapping around their knees, rode two abreast, chatting away oblivious to the big car behind them. Maynard nudged closer to their back wheels and jabbed his horn, a discordant cry that cut through the otherwise tranquil morning. The girls shrieked and wobbled towards each other, bumped elbows. And as he swung the car around them Maynard leant across Frank to yell out of the passenger window.

'Get off the road, Taylor!'

The nearest girl, blonde and red-faced, grinned back.

'Up yours!' she called.

As they pulled away with a throaty burst of engine, Maynard looked across at Frank and smiled.

The slightly raised eyebrow told Frank everything. So that's the kind of man you are, Frank thought: predictable.

'How long have you been on this kind of work?' Frank asked.

'Oh ages. From the start, really. I was on Project Rainbow in Fifty-eight. You?'

'I was at Cambridge then. Then I went to Saxby and

Barton Hall.'

Maynard nodded, apparently unsurprised at this information; did he already know Frank's background?

'You're still a young man,' said Maynard. 'How long have you been married?'

'Two years.'

'You'll have no regrets then. Not yet anyway.'

Frank didn't want to talk about women. If ever the subject came up with other men, he felt as if he were on the outside of things, ignorant of the insights and stratagems they so casually exchanged. Not that there was any big secret to understanding the other sex; the mystery lay in all those nuanced approaches taken by other men. Unsure how to reply to Maynard's provocative comment, Frank repeated one of his father's sarcastic catchphrases.

'I'm a lucky man.'

The closer they got the more the main reactor building receded from view behind an array of high fences, wooden huts and low concrete hangars. Below the razor wire the fences were punctuated by the usual warning signs.

Maynard wrestled the car into the short approach road and pulled up at the security barrier. Frank passed him his papers for the guard to see. A youth with a cluster of angry pimples around his left nostril, and a cap pulled low over his eyes, bent down to peer into the car. He gave Maynard a respectful nod then scrutinised Frank, his eyes lingering on the scar. Straightening, the youth stared at the small cropped photograph paperclipped to Frank's identification papers, then dipped his shoulders again to study again the newcomer. He raised a pink finger to his cheekbone, then drew a line down it.

'That new is it, sir?'

'It's rather an old photograph,' Frank replied, sensing Maynard's alertness to the exchange.

'Must have been a nasty wound that, sir. I've seen one like that, fresh, as it were. Worth getting a new photo, I'd say. The protocol is to check ID at every boundary. You don't want to have to keep explaining yourself.'

'Yes, thank you. I will.'

The youth handed Frank his papers and lifted the barrier. As Maynard rolled the car through the double gates, neither man said anything.

From the car park, Maynard led Frank into a labyrinth of industrial pipework, storage tanks and sheds of varying shapes and size. The concrete path was punctuated by colour-coded signs. Red arrows pointed to H5, blue arrows to T6 and so on. Maynard walked briskly, offering no explanation or commentary. Now and then he issued a curt greeting to someone walking towards them but didn't stop to introduce Frank. He probably wanted to be rid of this scarred intruder as quickly as possible. Frank, striding along behind, committed the route to memory and simultaneously tried to decipher the numbering system of the buildings.

Maynard stopped outside a cuboid building of red brick. In a parody of a child's drawing of a house, there were four equally-sized windows and a centrally-positioned door with frosted glass panels. To Frank the building looked less like a library, and more like a modern suburban dentist's surgery. On the dusty front step a cluster of pot-plants were wilting from heat and neglect.

'Here you are,' said Maynard. 'The Citadel. You have an appointment here I believe, in a few minutes? I usually have my lunch at 12.30 with a few of the chaps, if you fancy it. Mondays it's usually meatloaf.'

Thankful to be left alone, Frank took a few paces up the path, then turned slowly on his heel, taking in his surroundings. From here he could see nothing of the sea, nor the beach; only the relentless sun, bouncing off iron pipes and salt-whitened concrete. Glowing above him was the white mass of the reactor. None of his letters had mentioned an appointment. But now that he was here, had indeed been delivered here by that dullard, Frank was not surprised. Given all that had brought him here, it was entirely to be expected. Still, he found himself shuffling around like some petrified boy waiting outside the door of his headmaster. Twin beads of sweat raced down each of his temples. Compose yourself, man. The story is clear and simple. And if in doubt, keep your mouth shut.

The frosted-glass door moaned as he pushed it. Inside it was cool and dim. A secretary, middle-aged and pinched, sat at a desk writing out a birthday card. Frank waited with his hands in his pockets as she closed the card, slid it into the matching envelope and jabbed out her tongue to moisten the edge. As she licked, her eyes were steady and cool on him.

'I'm sorry, my dear,' she said eventually. Her voice had a lilting local accent that was rather at odds with her appearance. 'You'll be here for Mr. Parker.'

'Frank Banner.'

With that information, the secretary rose from her desk and disappeared through a door behind it. Save for the ticking of a clock, the room, and the building around it, was silent. Like that suburban dentist's surgery, the walls were decorated with tranquil watercolours. On a coffee table lay a pile of *The Engineer* magazines. Frank reckoned a tooth extraction might be less painful than what he was surely about to endure.

The woman reappeared, a manila envelope under her arm, and showed him through to an office that was even drabber than the waiting room. The room was dominated by a princely mahogany desk. Onto its green baize surface were pressed the long grey fingers of Mr Parker.

'Welcome, welcome. Come in, Frank,' Mr. Parker called across the room. A tall man in, Frank guessed, his early sixties, Parker was one of those career physicists for whom nuclear fission had come two decades after their best years. He was dressed in grey flannel, and the countless laboratory hours had long washed any colour from his skin. Only an unruly shock of white hair gave a hint of youthful vigour. Mr Parker extended a hand for Frank to shake, and his eyes danced nervously. There was a sense of formality to the situation that implied either Parker had forgotten about their previous meeting, or he had some bad news to deliver.

'Sit down,' he said, gesturing to a chair. And as he levered himself back into his own chair, Mr Parker winced. 'Knees,' he said when he saw that Frank had noticed. 'Blasted useless things. Would you believe I used to be All-England Badminton Champion three years running? What is the half-life of a knee I wonder? Pretty damn short I'd say.'

Frank mumbled his agreement while trying to steal a glance, upside-down, at the single piece of paper, closely typed, that lay on the desk in front of Parker.

'Thank you for coming to see me. Welcome back. I'm glad it's all worked out for you to be here. I do hope you'll enjoy it here, I think we are doing some very important work. Very important indeed. Vital work for the future. But I don't need to tell you that. You haven't just got off the train from Cambridge. I just wanted to...'

Parker's voice trailed off and a frown shadowed his face. He looked at the piece of paper and seemed to find courage from it. Frank, who had been sitting hunched, almost cringing, now straightened his back in readiness.

'When we last met we didn't really talk about...about your history. But there's no getting round it, I'm afraid. I have a report from your last place, Barton Hall, so I know something of what happened. The official version, anyway.' Parker paused to let those words hang in the air. 'Because of that you probably won't be surprised to learn that we're going to start you here on a probationary contract. Three months, then we'll review how you're finding it. Also the Authority has asked that you do a psychological assessment. I'm sorry, I know you've done them before. But, well, you can understand, can't you?'

Frank nodded, then shrugged. 'That's fine.'

Parker looked relieved, if a little disappointed. No doubt he'd been anticipating this exchange for some time, dreading it perhaps. How much did he know of what really happened? At the time it had been made clear that it was in no one's interests for the affair to be widely known. Yet in this line of work there was a report in triplicate for everything. If you so much as sneezed in an Active area, you had to write two hundred words about it.

'You know,' said Parker, 'there aren't many good men in your field. We need your experience, your brain. But you're a risk, given what happened. We can't have men that are – unstable.'

Frank heard someone laughing outside, a woman's pitch. It sounded like she was standing close to the door to Parker's office.

Carefully, slowly, Frank said, 'I just want to work.'

'It's a high-pressure environment; we all understand that. Comes with the job. Everyone reacts differently.'

There was a questioning tone to the older man's voice. Has the assessment started already? Frank wanted to ask. No, this fossil was just trying to tease out a reaction. To someone like Parker, someone who no doubt lived entirely within their brain, the kind of anger and violence that was indelibly cut into Frank's face was morbidly fascinating. It was physical, visceral, immediate. Parker was in the grip of fear, and he wanted to know more.

An image sprang into Frank's mind. The familiar one that visited him at night. Andrea, in the green dress, kneeling on his chest, her knees like two white cauliflowers, the demonic look on her awful face and the gleaming flick-knife in her gloved fingers. She'd held it so delicately, and as she sliced him her expression changed from demonic to that of luminous curiosity. He remembered feeling her pure hatred before blood seeped into his eyes and the shock got him.

'It's a fresh start for my wife and me,' Frank said brightly. 'It's a lovely part of the world.'

Again there was laughter just outside the door, and yet Parker didn't seem to notice. Was that receptionist eavesdropping on their conversation? No, that laugh didn't fit with her voice. Frank shifted on his seat. The scent of flowers cloyed the air, making him feel nauseous.

'Did you...did you hear that?' Frank said, inclining his

head towards the door.

Parker frowned. 'Hear what, sorry?'

'It sounded like... No, nothing, ignore me.'

Shut up, *shut up*.

'Yes, well,' Parker continued, still disappointed. 'I dare say it will feel very different to London. Frankly the remoteness suits some better than others. When times are tough I find it helps to remember that we have a keen sense of purpose here. Very keen.'

'I think I'll like it. The sea is so...' The laughter outside became louder, near-hysterical. Still Parker seemed not to notice. Distracted, Frank struggled to find the right word to express himself, '...so close.'

So close.

A familiar voice. Close to his ear, and yet at the same time it was clearly the same laughing woman behind the door.

'Yes it is. And my advice is simply to throw yourself into all the social life and extracurricular activities that go on. There's a bar here, a table-tennis table over near the cooling tanks, and I think there are ballroom dancing lessons going on somewhere. Not that these fellows will allow for a foxtrot.'

He tapped his knees and smiled. On seeing the other man's relief that the interview was over, something tightened in Frank. There was a horrible kindness in Parker's face. Frank sat staring, caught between the energy of Andrea's hatred and Parker's sickening condescension. At least she was honest. At least she was genuine. The room seemed to shrink inwards upon him. The laughter had stopped, replaced not by silence but by a grim drone. His chest burned.

'It's not easy...' he muttered. 'Not easy to...'

Control yourself. But these two words weren't his. They just lay trembling on the air.

The sour salt of blood on his tongue. Bruised flesh striping his knuckles. He had to get out of the room before he did something unwise. Grabbing his briefcase, Frank muttered goodbye and lurched towards the door.

Behind him he heard Parker call out: 'But my dear fellow, do you know where you're headed?'

• • •

The meatloaf was truly dreadful but no one else was complaining. Throughout his long and frustrating morning of safety briefings, form-filling and guided tours – during which he hadn't been offered a single cup of tea – he'd looked forward to lunch. At Barton Hall lunch in the canteen had been quite the social occasion and the food was excellent. Here it seemed different strategies would have to be employed. Tomorrow he would put a packet of chocolate digestives into his briefcase.

Maynard was telling him and Anthony, a regular lunch companion, about a chap whose neoprene gloves had punctured at the start of Maynard's shift, releasing plutonium into the atmosphere of the room they were working in. Three of them, including Maynard, had to traipse down to the Health Office for a test. All showed up as contaminated and were duly sent to the bathrooms to have a wash and blow their noses. Standard procedure. Forty minutes and a cup of tea later they were back at work.

Maynard held up a forkful of meatloaf and gazed at it

in mock horror.

'What's more dangerous? A slice of Shirley's meatloaf or a dose of plutonium?'

Anthony issued a little snort. 'Well if it's made from local cows you'll be getting a hit anyway. Those heifers are getting the full effect and they're starting to show the benefits. There's talk of a cow down near Huntsby that has five legs and calls himself Stanley.'

Maynard nodded his approval of Anthony's deadpan delivery. 'I hear he's hoping to get into Oxford next year to read Physics.'

'Let's hope he dodges Shirley's mincer before the interview,' Anthony said gravely, then looked at Frank in alarm. 'Crikey, you're not an Oxford chap are you?'

Frank shook his head, smiling. 'No, but my middle name is Stanley.'

The other men laughed at this and the atmosphere eased. He would be one of the lads, for now at least. Anthony was different to Maynard, though they seemed to be good friends. In contrast to Maynard's puggish, tough face – a face that could easily have belonged to an East End hoodlum – Anthony possessed a finer, more sensitive profile. He was perhaps a couple of years younger than Frank, tall, with his black hair long enough that he could pull it into a ponytail, secured with an elastic band – easier to tuck into the plastic caps he was obliged to wear in the chemistry lab. To sit in the canteen with the ponytail still in took some nerve. Frank had already noticed a table of builders nudging each other and laughing. Anthony was apparently oblivious – or didn't care.

Maynard said, 'It's worth getting contaminated just to go and see that Emma who works down there. The one on the bike this morning. She's twenty-two you know.'

Anthony leaned towards Frank and said in hushed tones, 'Maynard knows the age of every woman on this site. It's his hidden talent. Well, hidden from his wife at any rate.'

Shaking his head and laughing, Maynard said, 'Not true. I only know the women under forty. If I want a tired old matron who's had too many children, I can go home, can't I? Anyway, it's all right for you, isn't it?'

'What do you mean?' Anthony said, frowning.

'Well, you've got your lithe little local yokel, haven't you?' Maynard said, then turned to Frank. 'Anthony here has pulled another one of those health centre girls, Alice. Even younger than Emma isn't she? Credit where credit is due.'

Anthony smiled, but it looked strained. Perhaps Anthony didn't like his relationship with Alice bracketed with Maynard's more base pursuits.

• • •

That afternoon, during his tea-break, Frank took off his blue coverall, changed back into his own shoes and went for a wander. Just to see how far he got. His laboratory was close to the reactor piles, the most secret and potentially dangerous part of the site, and he was pleased to discover that his badges got him into all the interesting buildings around the place. He did not actually enter then, of course, because that would have meant changing his shoes again and putting on protective clothing, but it was good to know that for all Parker's trepidation, he'd been given full access. Walking slowly along the side of the turbine hall, he noticed a thin gravel path, dotted with weeds, running away towards the sea. The view was mostly obscured by a concrete generator shed, a jumble of pipework and the chain-link fence, but Frank was able to squeeze himself into a place where the tufts on top of the sand dunes were visible, and beyond was clear, shimmering blue space. He stopped, leant against a concrete wall and lit a cigarette. The ground under his feet trembled as the huge waste pipes filled, then flushed their contents out onto the beach.

The wind carried to him the sound of laughter – the same high note he'd heard from Parker's office, though faint, now it was further away.

The turbine hall emitted its reassuring machine hum. The wind wove around the buildings. And underneath, almost entirely smothered by all those other layers of noise, was the sound Frank wanted to detect.

Refined and intermittent and ruthless. It was there all right. A buzzing that could never be traced. At Barton Hall, when he'd foolishly tried to explain this idea of his to a senior officer, he'd been given a week's leave to pull himself together. You can't hear radiation, they told him. Don't be a fool. And yet he knew that he could. The buzzing, he now knew, was the radiation in the air. It was just a matter of tuning in.

Footsteps rung out on the path behind him. Click, click, stop. The wind fell away and left a tense silence. Just a worker on a cigarette break, he told himself. Do not look round. Do not look.

At first he'd been incredulous that no one else heard the radiation. Then he understood. No one else was listening; they were too scared. Fear closed their minds. These particles quivering in the air represented a curiously fickle magic. Harnessed correctly, it had great power. To light homes across the country, to keep factories and shipyards running. It could also be packed into a bomb that would flash its obliterating light across a landscape. The power to destroy in an instant. What Frank understood was that, whether your intent was good or ill, radiation made you stronger. It was only a case of mastering its power. He was not scared of it. Indeed the 'incident' at Barton Hall had proven to him that radiation made *him* stronger. He was receptive to its unique power. After all, hadn't he been contaminated just three days before he delivered a beating to that piss-streak boy?

Frank reached out his arm and cupped his palm as if to catch radiation falling from the sky. In the sunshine his skin was creased and white as paper. In the end, he thought, everything will burn. Everything was just...

There was still someone behind him. Closer now. Almost close enough to breathe on the back of his neck. He started to shake. His gut shrivelled.

Her presence was poisonous, tempting. So she'd followed him here... What did she want from him? Or, how could he use her? He tried to extinguish his fear. It was weakness. Nudged his feet around to the side, spun and...no. There was no one.

She was, after all, in prison.

He was still alone.

7

NEUTRINO

On the pavement outside the school Gail shifted from foot to foot, uneasy in her stiff (and bloody hot) wool suit and smart brown shoes. It was early, the first lesson of the day, and yet the sun bore down on her head, teasing out rivulets of sweat from her scalp. The interview was scheduled for ten o'clock. Looking at her wristwatch she saw one minute past. All you have to do, she told herself, is ring that bell on the gatepost. Then someone will come and unlock them. You'll be in, moving, talking. Nerves are perfectly natural in this sort of scenario.

Setonisle Primary School was a low brick building – Victorian, Gail guessed – surrounded by a lush garden and a formidable brick wall. A pair of heavy wrought-iron gates kept the little ones from making a bid for freedom. Very unlike the modern concrete buildings in which Gail had taught during the previous academic year. She knew that she should – theoretically – find this place attractive. It was everything she had hoped for, and yet those iron gates were somehow intimidating her.

Two more minutes ticked by. Now she was late. And still she couldn't reach up and ring that bell. All the old feelings of failure were reeling her back, siphoning away what scant confidence she had left. She was a mediocre teacher at best, prone to frazzle when faced with the required plate-spinning. Either she got too involved with the emotional problems of specific children, or she could barely remember their names. Her last head-teacher, an austere Scot called Mary Macdonald, had once attempted to give Gail a pep talk over a cup of Ovaltine, but all Gail could remember was the phrase, *this is harder than it looks*. It was going to be an excellent quote to support her imminent departure from the teaching profession. Very imminent.

She turned away from the gates and walked slowly back towards the village. Peeled off her jacket and folded it over her handbag. Lit a cigarette. Sod it. Unsure whether what she was feeling was crushing defeat or the exhilaration of release, she told herself that this was a time for cool thinking. Despite the weather, ha!

Frank had better get her pregnant. How she longed to have that little button of life inside her. It was to be her project for the autumn and winter. Falling pregnant now would mean a baby in late March. She and Frank hadn't been trying too seriously (he was typically reserved about the whole idea) and the attack had thrown them both well off-course. Now she hoped they might get into something of a routine; after all, wasn't it really just a numbers game? Like those pinball machines where you fire silver balls up a chute in the hope of ringing a bell at the top. The radiation was a worry though. Frank had never managed to convince her it was safe. His theory that it was indeed beneficial to health in small doses seemed ludicrous to her. Many of his colleagues at Barton Hall had children, and perfectly normal and lovely children they were too. And yet...many of the mothers of those children admitted to being scared during their pregnancies. What if the radiation caused physical deformity or mental deficiency? How much exposure did their husbands really get at work (they all knew their husbands lied about this), and could it permeate through to an unborn child?

Gail walked on, inhaling the dry salted air and marvelling at the way the intense heat seemed to soften every surface. It was as if the fabric of rigid structures, both physical and psychological, was being loosened. There was a hazy, buzzing, unreal quality to the morning. She felt a churning in her gut and thought for a moment she might be sick. A church bell rang across the houses.

• • •

Holding its stem between thumb and forefinger, Judy turned her glass of white wine, and gazed into its greenish tint. She looked pale and tired. A sheen of sweat clung to her temples. Inside the house the children were screaming at each other, but she paid them no attention.

Gail had not told her about her failure to visit the school, and yet Judy seemed somehow to understand what Gail wanted. Not that Judy was really saying what

Gail wanted to hear.

'I mean it's wonderful – don't get me wrong – but it's bloody lonely. Obviously you've got all the baby clubs and coffee mornings at the library and all of that, but how long do they last? And then you're back in the house again, staring at the same four walls. And the sleep, or lack of it. Oh, seriously, some days I really thought I was losing my mind. It's a kind of insanity, that level of sleep deprivation.'

'Didn't Maynard help?' asked Gail, knowing the answer.

'What do you think? He just grunted and pushed me out of bed. I've got work in the morning – that was his card – and anyway the kids didn't want him. They want their mummy.'

'Well, I'd like to say Frank will be different, but I'm not sure I'd really believe it myself.'

As a test she tried to imagine him bending over a cot, cooing their baby back to sleep. She couldn't conjure the image. Indeed it was hard enough to conceive what the child might look like. Having never been to the farm (the famous farm, site of so much of his terror) Gail had never seen any pictures of Frank as a child. He'd been, she could imagine, a serious child, always with a furrowed brow. Intelligent, focused, anxious.

'He's different, your husband. I like him,' said Judy, and she let this statement hang in the air for a few moments before continuing. 'Maynard is just an old-fashioned sexist pig. No different from his father, who was a complete bastard. Once tried to put his hand up my skirt.'

'Frank has his own problems,' Gail murmured. But Judy didn't seem to hear, and they fell silent for a time, each absorbed in the landscape of her own marriage.

Since the attack Frank had retreated even further into his shell of scientific detachment. Any conversation could become what he called 'simply a rational discussion', which seemed to her much like an argument, just without the shouting. It was tiresome. When she curled into him in bed, she could feel the tension across his shoulders. Her fingers had to work at pulling apart his clenched fists.

'I worry about that place,' Gail said. 'What it does to the men – to anyone who works there.'

Judy sighed. 'It makes them hard, that's what I think. Like...cruel, too scientific and logical about everything. They're scientists, right? They don't deal in emotions. It's all buried. I can't remember the last time Maynard said he loved me. I mean, really said it and meant it.'

Sometimes Frank woke in the night with an anguished yell. Sometimes she caught him staring at her and it was as if the Frank she knew and loved had departed, leaving only a husk of a man. And at these moments she couldn't help but remember what he'd done to that boy.

Gail knew her husband would never do anything to hurt her, but it didn't seem quite right that she had to tell herself so.

8

ELECTRON

Over the rest of that week the heat deepened, like washes of paint layered on to a wall. It felt different to summer in a city, Gail pointed out, as they sat on their patio one evening, drinking lemonade with ice cubes. Different because in a city the streets became choked and you felt as though you were under assault by the sun.

'Here,' she said, 'here, the land seems to come alive. When you walk through a field there is so much wildlife jumping about – bugs, butterflies, birds, wasps. It's so beautiful.'

Frank listened to her rambling accounts of exploring the marshes to the south and the network of villages inland, though the majority of her time seemed to be spent on the beach. She bore an arc of sunburn just below her hairline and her nose shone pink.

He wasn't jealous; he wouldn't swap the reactor core for the beach, even though his body didn't seem to be reacting well to the new job. Yesterday he'd had stomach cramps. Now every swig of lemonade aggravated the mouth ulcer he'd been nursing all day.

'The skies are just enormous here. I know that sounds like a daft thing to say,' Gail said, and he nodded, hardly listening. Mr Parker had not heard the laughter coming from beyond his door, so was it real?

Andrea is here with us, he wanted to say to Gail. She's followed us here. She won't let me go that easily.

'You should see the canteen,' he said instead. 'There's really a lot of choice.'

'I don't even really know what day it is,' she giggled.

His wife had a talent for time-wasting. Whole days could slip through her fingers and she felt no sadness or guilt. She had a dreamy soul, self-sustaining and naturally happy. It insulated her from the mundane problems of life; useful, until you enter the world of work. Wherever she worked – and there had been three different schools even in the short period he'd known her – Gail made friends. She attracted people because she sought to understand them, and made an effort to help them if she could. At the work itself, however, she was less successful. The gap between her idea of teaching and the reality was too wide.

Of course she wanted a baby. She was thirty-two and her dreamy soul had long been ready. A flimsy pretence of her getting a job in the village school had been constructed in the weeks leading up to their departure, but he knew her real plan. And Frank knew he would have to smash up his fear of becoming a father; there was no running away from that particular destiny.

He looked across at the power station, its outline hazy against a cream-coloured sky.

All week the place had been unbearably hot. The laboratories were furnaces. Ventilation was paltry, they weren't allowed to bring in temporary fans, and when you were obliged to wear as much clothing as a blasted astronaut...well, it was no wonder that people were fainting all over the place. Management shortened shifts in some sections and put great drums of drinking water in the changing rooms. Signs appeared warning of the increased risk of fires. The deputy head of Frank's department, a dour Welshman with a single thick eyebrow that ran right across his face, gathered everyone together to warn them that some materials might become volatile in such high air temperatures and, if in doubt, to speak to him. Was Frank being paranoid, or did he see his boss look at him when he said the word volatile?

Finishing one's shift and stepping into the fresh air was a blessed relief. Frank was in a team of six: four men and two women. They made a pretty decent effort to befriend him, asking lots of questions about his background, telling funny stories about the management and the locals, but Frank kept his distance. When they invited him to the bar one evening for a drink he told them his wife was ill at home with shingles. The work was interesting, difficult. Frank and his colleagues were collectively known as the PIE unit, for Post-Irradiation Examination. Their job was to extract fuel elements from the reactor piles, cut them up and look at them under the microscope. The elements had recently begun to show erratic behaviour and the hope was to better understand them. Everything was done in flasks, in shielded conditions.

'Gosh that Judy does like a drink,' said Gail. 'She's not really a very happy person, I'd say.'

That such small, drab lumps of metal could be so powerful still confounded and fired Frank's imagination. Everyone had a different way of coping with the danger; at least that's what he'd been told during his initial training at Barton Hall. The fear they drummed into you at that place.

Frank had kept quiet. He knew the history of radiation. He'd heard the stories of early pioneers dying in agony and the fate of the American playboy who drank three bottles of radiation tonic a day, until his jaw fell off. And yes, surely if you paid no heed to proper dosage, and knew nothing of what you were dealing with, poor results would follow. Frank, however, was no fool. He believed in radiation like some people believed in vitamins. There was plenty of evidence if you looked in the right places. The body could absorb and process very specific quantities, and grow stronger.

'She really struggles with little Lucy; she's quite the rebel. She told me that the other day Lucy got out all of Judy's nail polishes, decided to paint her toenails and got nail polish all over the carpet. That certainly won't come out. Not in a million years.'

There was a man in Frank's unit at Seton – a family man by all accounts – named Bob, whose face betrayed fear every time he stepped into the reactor. To be close to him was to be unnerved. Frank wanted him out. That kind of fear was irreversible and infectious. It posed a risk to the rest of them. When working with these materials one had to be precise and confident. The worst accident that had happened at Barton Hall during Frank's time there happened because of someone with shaky hands.

•••

The next day, at the end of his shift Frank changed back into his cotton trousers and shirt-sleeves, issued a swift goodbye and walked, quick and lightfoot, towards the gates. The work was physically tense and cramped, and their clothing wasn't designed for movement, so to be able to walk freely, swinging one's briefcase in long arcs, was a tremendous release. Through the car park he kept his eyes firmly forward to avoid encountering Maynard.

Walking across the meadow, that burst of pent-up energy soon dissipated. He moved over the cracked earth, letting the scenes of his day play across his mind. In the distance was his strange new house. Above it the immense melting sun. Sometimes he tried to picture what the Hiroshima explosion had looked like from space; just a small white flash on the surface of an insignificant planet. The seed of its eventual self-destruction. Gail would be waiting for him, brim-full of her day, utterly uninterested in whether he'd cheated death that day, made a breakthrough in the lab, or come home so contaminated his socks were glowing. She would talk at him, giggling nervously all the time, until he was forced to lock himself in the bathroom.

But no, Gail wasn't there. Just like the day before. A scrawled note left on the kitchen table told him that she was *Over the road! Come over!* He did not. Instead he had a bath, a cup of tea and got on with the unpacking (which they'd agreed Gail would do but that plan seemed to have been conveniently forgotten). Living out of boxes was annoying as hell. When Gail did finally come home she stank of gin, and indeed was too drunk to cook dinner.

On Friday morning, the end of his first week on the job, Frank remembered that among the things he'd wedged into the small shed in the back garden was his old bicycle. It was a heap of rust really but just wheeling it across the garden reminded Frank of how much he'd enjoyed flying around the Oxford streets during the early summer evenings.

After an uneventful day at work – the heat seemed to have worn everyone out to such a degree that they did the minimum possible work – Frank pulled his machine from the bicycle racks and set off along the coast road, away from his house. Pushing hard on the pedals for ten minutes or so, he was soon clear of the power station. Its incessant hum was replaced by the eddying breeze rushing around his ears. The sun warmed his back. This was the life. Freedom. How far north could he go? Where would the road end?

Frank, however, was not in great physical shape. The effort began to catch up with him, and as the road gently curved along behind the sand dunes, he eased up. The sea was visible only in glimpses, but the wind carried its salty tang to him. The empty lane shone like glass.

At a gap between two high dunes he came to a stop, dismounted and laid the bicycle on its side in the sand. Dumped his briefcase, which he'd been carrying on a strap around his shoulder, alongside the bicycle. It contained nothing more important than a few melting chocolate digestives and some mint imperials.

As far as he could see in both directions, the beach was deserted. Out at sea, a cargo ship nudged the horizon.

Almost without conscious thought, pulled by some temptress of the deep, Frank unbuttoned his shirt.

The water was electrifyingly cold. The moment that his body was fully submerged it seemed to harden and become immobile. For a few panicky seconds he feared no movement was possible for these stone limbs, and that he'd sink to the seabed just a few feet below. But then his arms stiffly grabbed and pulled, and his legs flapped then kicked, he caught a breath and sensed forward motion. That most wonderful thing. The sheer impossibility of swimming in that vast ocean. The madness of it. He was an atom. Less than an atom, for he was easier to destroy. But atoms did not feel such joy, such immediate physical exhilaration, from the water caressing his balls, and the slice of his fingers into the crystalline blue. He was a good swimmer. Somehow it had always been present in his life. He'd often found opportunities to thrash up and down an indoor pool or a lido, and on seaside holidays he was a wave-watcher. He knew the power of riptides, but if it looked safe he'd be striding off down the beach while Gail dozed behind her dark glasses.

There was no danger here, as far as he could tell. The water was calm. He swam away from land without any current nagging his legs. Why not do this every Friday evening over the summer? Wasn't this part of the reason for moving here? He felt alive, in a balanced, slow way. Nothing bad could happen now. After a couple of minutes of looking out across the purple-blue horizon, he stopped and turned around, treading water with lazy jellyfish strokes. And as he turned, in the corner of his vision he saw a figure on the beach, small and still. His name came lapping over the waves, *Frank, Frank*, and the woman dissolved into the dunes. The temperature of the water dropped and his muscles tensed. The void beneath his pathetic waggling legs was overwhelming in its power. Utter indifference, that's what the natural world offered. Life, death, who fucking cared. She knew that.

Naked, Frank lay on top of a sand dune and let the wind sweep over him. The sun plucked moisture from his skin. The sand was hot under his shoulder-blades. Closing his eyes, he saw swimming colours, pink and blue. The thrill of such enveloping sensation. The brilliance of the light.

A barbaric beating. I would expect you to show deep and unconditional remorse, and yet I see none. It was funny when other people told you how you should feel. How futile. Altering someone else's feelings was as impossible as stopping the incoming tide. Really though, the judge was trying to convey his horror and moral outrage on behalf of decent society. That was his job, right? It wasn't so much the act itself as Frank's reaction to what he'd done. Witnesses said that when he straightened up, leaving the boy to bleed all over the pub floor, Frank laughed and laughed and laughed. It was this laughter that so frightened the crowd and made them back away, allowing Frank time to stumble out of the pub and away into the night.

So did he feel shame? No.

Guilt? No.

Only – and this was weeks later – a kind of scientific curiosity about what had happened inside his brain that night, and a wonder at its destructive power. Wasn't there a simple beauty in destruction? To strip something down, shatter the veneer that society demanded. Certainly.

Another phrase of the judge's stuck in his mind: *Use*

your work for the greater good. You have the potential to save, to renew, to protect. Put this behind you and focus on that. And with that he was free. A suspended sentence, to gasps of shock from the public gallery. Then came the screaming from the boy's family. But Frank was already walking out into the Oxford street, where rain swirled in the air and buses grumbled.

A daft thing for the judge to say, when one thought about it; after all, wasn't he doing exactly that – protecting poor Karen and her unborn baby? Not that she'd shown much bloody gratitude. Quite the opposite in fact. Still, she was young. In time she would see what he'd done for her, and come to thank him. He was confident of that.

Frank dragged his fingers through the sand and poured some onto his belly. Flexing his fingers, he looked at his knuckles, marvelling that they could do so much damage to a person's face. Quite incredible. He could still feel the boy's cheekbone cracking, the soft cartilage of his ear, the strands of spittle that clung to Frank's fist as it reeled back from the boy's mouth. That blood-red fury seemed to sit somewhere between and behind Frank's eyes, directing his limbs with calm and precise messages. It had been a very satisfying exercise.

9

PHOTON

What fools we make ourselves for men, Alice thought as she pulled lipstick across her mouth. It was cheap stuff: Boots' own. Her friend Susan had Estée Lauder, a big box of it from that Ipswich department store, but then Susan had snagged herself a chunky fisherman who liked to splash his cash on a Saturday afternoon.

Not for Alice. She wasn't going to swim into that lobster pot. Sure, it was attractive enough at first, but the future was all too predictable: get married in the chapel and try not to look at the memorial boards that listed all those lost at sea, have a baby or four, get fat, watch your husband drink himself into a lumbering wreck, wonder how life slipped through your fingers. Alice had seen it all before. Her older sister, for one.

No, not for Alice. She was different and she was going to hold onto that. Hold tight for dear life. Was that the sound of his little car on the lane outside? She felt a blush of self-disgust as she pictured him clambering out and opening the front gate. Anthony was proof that men did not necessarily lose their awkwardness with age. Bless him. He was sweet but, well, no more than that.

Initially she'd been attracted to the idea of an older, intelligent man. Soon enough she'd realised that was the problem – she was attracted to the *idea* of such a man, not to Anthony. He had both those qualities, yet utterly failed to excite her. For several weeks she'd been considering giving him the push. The only thing that had stopped her was his almost casual mention of the possibility of a transfer to Bristol where some new facility was being built.

There might be a job down there for me, he'd said – a promotion. And Bristol is lively, there's a great scene down there (Anthony was a jazz enthusiast). We could live in the city and drive out to the power station together every day.

The way he described Bristol made it sound like New Orleans.

Hence the self-disgust. Would she really move halfway across the country with a man she did not love?

Well, yes. Maybe. How else would she escape this fish-pond of a village? Her original plan, to go to university, had been scuppered by a boy, that little runt from Fothersham who broke her heart a week before her A-levels. So the nuclear industry was her plan B. She was doing well at the health centre, her boss liked her, but she was too low in the hierarchy to request a transfer. She needed a man.

Unfortunately.

As she stood up she smoothed down her ever-so-sensible skirt. He hadn't said as much, but Alice guessed Anthony would want her to look as grown-up as possible for this dinner. What was the life of a scientist's wife? Dinner parties, exchanging recipes and childcare tips, assessing each other's husbands?

Alice had promised herself she would be good tonight. A nice girl. Now though, picking up her clutch bag from the dressing table in the room where she'd slept these last twenty-two years, she felt a tingling rush of rebellion.

• • •

Gail wiggled his tie then fixed him with one of her looks.

'Come on, it won't be that bad. You'll be fine.'

'There's nothing to talk about. I've got nothing to say to these people.'

She gave a little exasperated sigh. 'Well Maynard and Judy have got enough to say for the rest of us put together. And you like Anthony don't you? Is that his name? I keep forgetting.'

She turned to the mirror by the front door and flounced her hair. He was doomed, utterly doomed. A dinner party. Hours of awkwardness, of fixing a smile on his face that would make his jaw ache, of listening to those bores, of trying to live up to Gail's billing – oh, he's really funny you know, when you get to know him, he's just, well, *shy*.

'Come on grumpy guts, you might even enjoy yourself.'

I will fucking not, Frank did not say.

There were perhaps twenty paces between their front door and the bungalow across the road. Twenty paces to feel the sun on one's face and to inhale the air that brimmed with pollen and salt. The wind tugged at Gail's skirt, pressing blue satin against the curve of her hip. Her heels sank into the warm tarmac.

Judy opened the door and put a finger to her lips.

'Maynard is just putting the little darlings to bed,' she said in an exaggerated stage whisper. 'Come in, come in. Shoes off if you don't mind.'

They followed her through the house, which was laid out exactly as theirs was, yet seemed much smaller because of the clutter that filled every room. The hallway was so full of coats and wellington boots and umbrellas and school bags that it was quite a negotiation just to get the front door shut. Further in there were pieces of Meccano underfoot, dolls staring up from dark corners, piles of scribbled-on paper and, on a chair in the kitchen, a heap of washing. Steam from three rattling saucepans drifted out through the back door.

'Ignore the mess,' Judy called as she dived behind the hob and armed herself with a wooden spoon. 'I'm sure you'll take us as you find us. Drink?'

She produced a bottle of gin and three glasses. Out on the patio, drinks fizzing in their hands, Frank and Gail surveyed the detritus of family life. An empty paddling pool, footballs, piles of sticks, a wooden horse on wheels. Around the lawn a few small shrubs were trying to make a home.

'Believe it or not, I used to be a very tidy person,' Judy said. She was standing close to Frank, gazing out at the garden, and her voice was calm, almost thoughtful. 'But then you have children and that all goes out of the window. You get to the point where if everyone is dressed and no one has vomit or chocolate or milk on them, you're happy.'

Frank wondered how much Gail had told Judy about her own campaign for children. And whether she thought him to blame for their failure. When Maynard appeared his face was heavy with sleep. In an effort to get Lucy to sleep he'd lain down with her and nodded off himself. Seeing Gail seemed to perk him up though. His comments about her dress were a little too rapturous, and sent his wife, rolling her eyes, away into the kitchen.

Alice and Anthony arrived half an hour late, but apparently didn't feel the need to apologise. Though his tie was demure grey, Anthony's suit was so brightly blue it hurt one's eyes to look at it for too long. Alice was small and slender with brown hair that hung in waves below her shoulders. She was suntanned but it seemed her skin had a naturally dark tone.

Thankfully, Frank had never had cause to go down to the health centre, so he hadn't met Alice. At lunch – over the last two weeks their canteen meeting had now become a regular appointment – Anthony said little about this girl of his, other than that she was the daughter of a boat-builder, and that she was ambitious, dreamt of living in London or even abroad, of having a career of her own and not being tied down by family.

'Maynard? Maynard? Can you help me please?' Judy called from the kitchen. Maynard smiled and went inside, to where his wife was dashing about in a way clearly designed to attract attention. Frank, sensing trouble, followed and stood by the back door, leaning on the door-frame and sipping his gin and tonic.

Maynard stood with his back to Frank, partly hiding

Judy, but Frank could still hear her hissing, 'Stop it, just stop it.'

'What?'

'You know very well. Leering at her. It's pathetic.'

'Judy, shut up. You're drunk.'

Frank stepped into the kitchen. He wanted them to think he might have heard, especially Maynard.

'Can I help at all?'

They reeled around and for a moment there was silence. Maynard's cheeks flushed.

'No, no, you go and enjoy the sunshine,' said Maynard in a forced jolly tone. 'She's just got herself in a bit of a tizz. I'll get it all sorted.'

Wielding a cucumber, Judy glared at him. 'Darling?'

'Yes?'

'Shut the fuck up, I'm sure Frank helps his wife around the house. Perhaps he even does some cooking now and then. And I'm sure Gail doesn't see it as diminishing his manliness, as you seem to.'

Frank tried not to laugh. Maynard forced a laugh, but looked ruffled. Frank imagined that Maynard didn't like being shown up in front of other men.

'I help. I put the children to bed didn't I?'

Judy turned and stepped over to Frank, grabbed his upper arm in her plump red fingers. Her grip was as strong as the imploring look in her eyes. The smile fell from Frank's lips as her obvious loneliness rushed up at him.

'Frank dear, promise me one thing. When your lovely wife has your babies, don't be a prize cock, like my husband. She deserves better than that.'

• • •

Gail watched, fascinated, the impact of this younger woman on the men around the table. She was just a girl really, full of that serene arrogance that comes from never having failed, never having felt the bruises of disappointment. There was a languor to the way she moved that suggested latent vitality, like an athlete at rest. This, no doubt, the men would be feeling in terms of sexuality, though there was more to it than that. By her languor Alice was implying strength, by her quietness she was implying thought, by her demure clothes she was implying that she didn't need to flaunt her body to attract these men.

Maynard's eyes kept flicking back to Alice. Usually this happened when his wife was talking. With every glance he seemed to absorb some new detail. He's a simple man, Gail thought. An engineer who probably considers himself an expert on women's bodies. The kind of man who compares and ranks women by their breasts. A predictable brute with no more depth than the waves that lapped at this strangely empty piece of coast. Still, she supposed, there is a place for such men.

Gail made herself splutter (no one seemed to notice) as she told herself, I bet he'd get you pregnant quick as anything.

Ridiculous thought!

Alice wanted escape, not babies. That much was clear from the faces she pulled when the conversation turned to the village. Did she see Anthony as her hero, rescuing her from an interminable fate? Was she already suggesting he transfer to another power station (not that the others were exactly located in thriving metropolises – the only real choice was which section of bleak, windswept British coastline you preferred). Perhaps just getting out of Setonisle would be enough for Alice. Poor Anthony. So gormless. So keen to make everyone laugh that eight out of ten of his jokes missed their mark. Did he know he was being used? Did he care? Among men, possession (for they would see it that way) of a younger woman, especially one so coquette, was prized. Maynard's jealousy came off him like steam on a frozen day.

And Frank? Not an obvious drunk, Frank nevertheless took pleasure in alcohol's great capacity for softening up the world. Gail pictured his mind as a machine, whirring constantly, working close to its limit, just the right side of breakdown. Alcohol slowed the machine, gave him some rest. Accordingly there were physical signs that Gail had grown used to spotting; his speech slurred a little, he sank down into chairs, his eyelids grew heavy. It was possible to rouse him – Gail had her techniques – to a kind of giggly playfulness, a side of her husband other people rarely saw, and one she loved very much.

Right now she could see the gin exerting itself on his senses. His attention was drifting, he looked sleepy. When she returned to the table, having passed out plates and done many bustling trips to and from the kitchen, Judy had nudged her chair closer to his. An unconscious movement? Was she genuinely attracted to Frank or was it merely a pointless attempt to make her husband jealous? Alice couldn't stop herself staring at Frank's scar. Once, as her gaze travelled its length, her lips parted. Over the past months Gail had seen that line of horror change from blood that seeped, to blood that congealed into sticky dark lumps, to raw new tissue attempting to close the wound, sometimes ripping and letting more blood ooze out, and she felt only revulsion for it. She didn't want to, and knew she had to accept it, that love and marriage demanded she force back the nausea that often bloomed in her chest, but the disgust ran deep into her. So it amused and bewildered her when other women gazed at Frank's disfigured features and seemed to stir with lust. Perhaps they imagined that in being cut open Frank had been able to see inside himself. Perhaps Alice wanted to place her fingers on his cheek, either side of the pink corded track and start pulling, tearing that tender new tissue apart, prising him open.

For his part Frank paid the girl scant attention. Much as he hated his father, Frank had inherited from him a rather quaint paternalistic position towards young women. Rather than trying to fuck Alice, as Maynard was surely plotting, Frank would only want to protect her. Given recent events this was worrying in itself.

• • •

'So are you feeling settled in yet?' Alice asked Gail as they set to work on their poached salmon and fried potatoes.

'Oh yes, though I do need to find something to do while Frank's at work,' Gail replied. 'Sitting on the beach is fine for now, but this weather won't last forever.'

'Gail went to see the headmistress at the school, about a job,' said Frank. Since meeting Gail he'd been dragged to innumerable occasions like this – she was incapable of saying no to an invitation, even to people she didn't like.

And he'd developed something of a technique for coping; he behaved as a kind of deflector, contributing to the conversation but at the same time sending the attention elsewhere. It made him look modest and self-effacing, and stopped him saying the things that were running through his head.

Judy gasped. 'Oh really? How wonderful that would be. You'd be looking after Lucy and William.'

'Oh well it might not happen…'

'I'll talk to her,' interrupted Judy. 'She listens to me. She knows I've got experience on a PTA and she's often said how much she values my opinion. I'll put in a word for you.'

Perhaps sensing Gail's discomfort, Alice said, 'In the meantime, you can just enjoy the sunshine. I'm jealous.'

'It's amazing to have such lovely beaches so close, and I have them virtually to myself,' said Gail.

'What, you go and sit on the beach during the day, while we're at work?' asked Maynard, pretending to be scandalised.

Gail waved her fork in a carefree manner, sending a grain of rice flying across the table. 'Absolutely, why live at the seaside if you're not going to enjoy it? I put on my swimming costume, pack a book, and lie in the sand dunes, trying to cook myself. It's heavenly.'

'Bloody hell. Well, good on you,' said Maynard. Frank knew the idea of Gail lying alone in the sand dunes in her swimming costume was pulsing through Maynard's mind. He saw an image of Maynard standing over Gail as she lay prone and vulnerable with her eyes shut.

A woman's voice whispered through his head, soft and teasing. *He's vicious – vicious.*

No one was near him. No one was talking to him. The conversation was prattling on around him. He shuddered, felt suddenly light-headed. Where had the voice come from? Was it the drink?

No, come on, you know who that is, he told himself.

And Maynard's eyes were on him, sneering at him. I can take her from you, that look was saying. I would only need to snap my fingers. Just like Frank's father: that same violent arrogance, the assumption that he would always get his way. Bully his wife, sleep around, strike his children. Why did men behave so? Frank had chosen a different path, and men like Maynard hated him for it.

'I never think of us living at the seaside, as you put it,' Alice was saying. 'I always think of piers and candy-floss and silly postcards and all that.'

Judy nodded. 'It rather felt like a holiday when we first arrived too, though it doesn't last. Especially when you've got the little ones in school.'

'If you need something to do, why not join the lifeboat crew?' chimed Anthony. Everyone ignored him. Despite, or perhaps because of, the idiotic jokes, Frank couldn't help liking Anthony. There was a puppy-like quality to him, always looking to please, to get a laugh. It was also a defence mechanism, of course. Occasionally, if you caught him off-guard, it was possible to sense a childish vulnerability, and in Maynard's company there was always that school-playground dynamic of leader and led.

'Are you a football man or a rugby man, Frank?' said Maynard.

'Neither,' Frank replied.

'Frank likes to run, he used to be a champion at cross-country,' Gail said, and then she pumped her arms back and forth, grinning like a lunatic.

Anthony nodded. 'Ah, very good, the splendid isolation, the wind in one's hair, the nobility of pain...'

'I eat far too many biscuits now to be able to run fast enough to feel the wind in my hair, though there's certainly plenty of pain,' Frank replied, after he'd forced down a chunk of overcooked salmon.

In truth, he hadn't gone for a run in over a year. In company, Gail often referred to his 'running', sometimes going as far as implying that he could have represented his country in competition if only he'd been bothered. It was touching, and bemusing. She seemed to like the inferences people drew from this article of news, that her husband was an interesting loner, that he liked an ascetic sport, that he was different to rugby-playing louts like Maynard.

'I'd say you'd be pretty fast yourself, with that fist-pump action,' Maynard said to Gail, smiling.

Judy rolled her eyes. 'Oh dear. I'm sorry, his flirting really is so adolescent.'

'I find that true of most men,' Gail said, looking at Judy then Alice, the latter smiling back so vaguely it was clear she hadn't been listening.

'Maynard pursued me for absolutely ages, like for yonks. Relentless he was. I just wasn't fussed.'

'What changed?' asked Alice, suddenly interested.

'I saw him in his swimming trunks,' Judy replied, trying and failing to stay deadpan. 'Those shoulders – oh, I was in love!'

Maynard beamed. 'They are superb, even if I do say so myself.'

A pair of fighter airplanes droned overhead, heading inland. Frank imagined himself up in the thin air, God-like, casting his gaze upon the specks of humanity below. He wondered how the power station looked from up there? Did the air around it shimmer? Did its discharge light up the ocean like a continent of phosphorescent fish?

He found that his eyes kept being drawn back to Alice. He didn't know her well enough to be able to judge whether her quietness was typical, but he was fascinated by the way her eyes kept drifting up to the sky. At those moments she was elsewhere, not listening, not caring for the conversation.

Beside Frank, Judy was looking under the table, at his tapping leg. She reached down and laid her hand on his knee, pressed firmly to stop the movement.

'My goodness, you're very tightly wound aren't you my dear?' she said, quietly, perhaps hoping the others wouldn't hear.

'Judy, leave the poor man alone,' her husband admonished.

'I just worry about you boys and the effect that place has on you,' Judy said with a shrug, though not removing her hand from Frank's knee. 'Maynard has the most awful nightmares you know. Wakes up in a cold sweat, can't get back to sleep for hours sometimes. Isn't that right, darling?'

While Maynard stared at his wife, Frank tried to work out if Gail could see that Judy's hand was on his leg. Gail looked pissed; her eyes were trying to focus on each of their faces. In the corner of her mouth was a smear of salad cream. Frank turned his fork between his fingers. He wanted to take a quick jab at Judy's hand. Move fast enough and he'd get enough thrust to get those prongs right through her hand. Hell, he might even puncture his own leg in the process, and then her blood would run into his own.

'Could I just use your toilet please?' he said.

She slipped the hand away. 'Of course darling, on the left by the front door. I'm sorry, have I embarrassed you?'

'No, only yourself,' came the reply from across the table.

Feeling rather pissed himself now that he was on his feet, Frank staggered through the house, kicking toys out of his path. It was only in the hallway that he remembered the two children asleep, and that he ought to be quiet. All the doors were closed. Two on the left, two on the right. He opened the first door on the left, slowly, in case the little darlings lay within. No, the warm glow from a bedside lamp showed him Maynard and Judy's bedroom. He went in and closed the door behind him.

It was tidier than the rest of the house, though the bed had been made in a hurry, and under the pool of light on the bedside table there was a glass of water with a lipstick-marked rim. The air was close and still. So this was where they fucked. If indeed they did fuck. He tried to imagine it, the stench of it, the grunts. Animal attacks animal. Nausea swelled in his chest, pushed up into his throat. When you stopped to think about it, the whole act was sickening. He considered what would happen were he to throw up all over their bed and turn over the sheets. The smell of it, their drunken disgust when they found his deposit. Then he considered what would happen if he took out his cock and pissed all over the bed. No doubt all hell would break loose if they worked out who was to blame – but would they dare confront him? The funny thing was that society would condemn him for such an action, relatively harmless as it was, and yet he was willing to bet that if he took a Geiger counter to that wardrobe in the corner, it would go off in a clicking frenzy. Maynard might be slowly poisoning his family but because radiation was invisible, that was all right. Madness.

As he turned to go he caught sight of a figure on the other side of the room. A bent, craven figure. Just his reflection in a full-length mirror. He stood looking at himself, disgusted by his ugly, broken face, dismayed by his slovenly posture. Christ, what a mess, he thought as he left the bedroom.

In the dark hallway he saw her. A wraith with eyes flashing as she moved. She was going into the children's bedroom. Horror scissored through him. The darkness swirled and roared. He lunged after her, but in his blind panic lost his footing and tumbled to the floor. Scrabbling to get to his feet, he saw her again. Bare feet, short and broad, squat calves, the hem of a blue dress. Judy.

'No need to fall at my feet,' she said, and pulled him up. But she did not release his hand and they stood facing each other, held in a moment of electric shock. His mind began back-pedalling, attempting to shed the image of the woman in the green dress, to slough off the clenching terror it had sent through him.

'You're different aren't you?' she said.

The appearance of that wraith, impossible as it was, had changed something, though he couldn't tell precisely what. He felt emboldened to say what was in his head.

'Do you hate him, your husband?'

She let go of his hand. 'I would be careful about saying that sort of thing.'

The others had moved to the living room and Maynard was putting on a record. With a scratchy jump a jazz drum began to reverberate around the room. Judy gave a yelp and grabbed Frank's hand. A saxophone note rose and she yanked his hands into the air. Still numb, confused by what he thought he'd seen in the corridor, Frank swayed with the music, his eyes struggling to focus.

A grin spread across Judy's face, and he followed her movements because that was all he could do. Her feet described tight circles in the carpet while her hips swung loose. More volume, more sloshes of gin, the rolling beat. The music was colour washing over him.

The dancing grew wilder. Gail's white throat as she threw her head back, Maynard's words seeping like gas into her ear. Alice demure and self-contained as she danced, yet flashing provocative looks in Maynard's direction. Then her hand finding his and her body spinning, the pleats of her skirt wrapping his shins.

Frank was spinning, fingers pulling him around faster and faster, faces contorted into lunatic laughter flashed past, and now Andrea came into view once more. She was in the room with them all, slipping in and out of the frame, bursts of green from her dress flipping around her knees, glints of light on the blade of her knife.

Her cold fingers intertwined with his, pulled him close so that she could whisper again, *He's vicious, that one – vicious. You watch.*

Frank snatched back his fingers and stumbled to the door colliding with a coffee table and sending a pile of books to the floor. Swinging out of the living room, he saw two people at the other end of the hallway, silhouetted against the harsh kitchen lights, their figures apart but close, and Maynard's hand sitting snug in the small of Alice's back. Frank stopped in the darkness of the hallway, held his breath, felt the alcohol inflame his nerve endings. He was looking down a black tunnel, its edges fuzzy but the image at its end pin-sharp. They had stepped into the kitchen now, the blueish light poured over them as they turned to face each other, his lips moving, her eyes creased with laughter. There was a strip of light between them like a lightning bolt.

Andrea was right. Maynard was dangerous. Frank didn't have time to question where she'd come from; something had to be done.

He moved quickly, silent and light on his feet, and in the same breath that they registered his approach he was upon them. He barged between them, carrying his momentum and dipping his left shoulder so as to knock Maynard out of the way. But Maynard was a big man, and not easily displaced. The collision sent Frank and Alice spinning across the room. He managed to stay upright, but crashed into the hob, dirty saucepans and serving spoons clattered to the floor, while Alice flew after him, helplessly off-balance, fell against some kitchen drawers and ended up sprawled on the floor.

Heavy breathing. The smell of stale cigarette smoke and white wine and fish. The two men staring down at the woman who now lay between them. Her skirt was ruffled in her lap, showing the whiteness of her thighs, and she was propped on one elbow, neck tilted at an odd angle, her eyes wild on Frank.

'What the hell are you doing?' she said between

lungfuls.

Frank straightened himself and began wiping fish sauce from his sleeve.

'What the hell?' she yelled.

'You don't understand,' he said, unable to articulate that he had rescued her. He felt that old disgust as he looked at her lying there beneath him. There were flecks of food in her hair. Her chest was heaving. Frank turned his gaze to Maynard, but the other man had eyes only for Alice's legs.

'I'm hurt,' she said. With a groan she pulled herself into a sitting position and leant forward to study her knees. There was indeed blood oozing from a gash there. 'See? Blood. Real blood.'

There was petty spite in her voice – that of a petulant little girl – but in her eyes he could see that she understood her power. This situation amused her, lying apparently helpless between two men. She reached out a hand to Frank but he ignored it.

By now Judy and Gail had arrived and were standing at the threshold of the kitchen, gaping as they tried to take in what they were seeing. Anthony loomed above them, his head craning forward as he leered.

Maynard slid his fingers into Alice's and in one unsteady movement the girl got to her feet. Somewhere behind a closed door a child started crying.

• • •

'So come on, how did he get that scar, really?' Alice asked. They were in Anthony's car, trundling along under the huge black sky, and she was warm with alcohol.

'I know as much as you do,' Anthony replied miserably. She didn't care to probe. His jealousies were his own problem.

'Someone cut him,' she said. 'Definitely. There was a man in the village like that, few years back. Had a scar right across his face. Only a knife will do that. He's a strange one though, eh?'

'That's my friend you're talking about.'

'God you're in a grump aren't you? Come on, you've got to admit he's a bit strange. You can see it in his eyes. Scary, they are.'

Anthony pulled a scornful face. He was always doing that to her; like she talked rubbish; like she was thick. Oh so superior he was. Well, if he thought he was going to park up by the dunes and have a fool around, he had another think coming.

But no, he didn't suggest stopping. Took her straight home. And no kiss goodnight either. Just a stony face. She could only imagine the turmoil going on in his head. He loved her yet she remained elusive, forever just slightly out of reach. Poor boy. Alice shrugged as they sat outside her house, the engine of that silly little car idling.

'It didn't mean anything – what happened tonight. Nothing. I was just having a bit of fun. A girl's entitled to wind up randy old men, isn't she? I'm not interested in Maynard. I'm with you, aren't I?'

But they both knew that the foundations of this speech were shaky. Anthony said nothing, so she got out of the car and watched him drive away into the village. Back to his immaculate bungalow and his novels about goblins and dragons. She'd never met anyone quite like Anthony; one day he'd make someone a good solid husband. Bloody infuriating though.

All the way home she'd been holding in her mind an image, holding it like precious cargo to be unwrapped in a safe place and examined carefully. It was a moment from the dinner party. Gail had been looking at Frank. It came just after Maynard said something cruel to put Frank in his place, ridiculing Frank's opinion on some boring subject, and rather than stand up for himself Frank had just gone quiet, seemingly drifted off into his own little world. And when Gail had looked at her husband she wasn't disgusted with his spinelessness, she looked at him so tenderly, so lovingly that it took Alice's breath away.

Alice felt drawn to Gail. Here was a woman to admire. She was handsome, mature and sexy in an understated kind of way. Confident. And she was ready to be a mother. That much was clear. More than ready... Old Frank looked exhausted with all the action he was getting.

In the village, the men were really just boys. No – worse than that – they were just fools. They believed you had to stand up for yourself or be emasculated. But it was utter bollocks. In that single loving look from Gail, Alice had sensed a world outside the village, a world of more complicated thought patterns, of people who did not accept that life was simple. This was where she belonged. If, in ten years' time, some young girl looked at her, Alice, and admired the subtle way she'd handled some awkward situation, well that was all right with her.

The alleyway running up the side of her house was pitch black. Above the rooftops of the sleeping cottages the heavens were veined with moonlight. Having grown up by the sea she wasn't even aware of its smell; the only scent she noticed now was the honeysuckle in the hedge.

Something silvery darted past her ankles, making her jump. Next door's cat. The little fucker. Alice hissed into the darkness.

Then she heard the crunch of a footstep on stones, behind her. She spun on her heel, expecting to see a figure framed in the entrance of the alleyway. But there was no one. Another noise, this time harder to place, like a grunt, carried on the thin breeze. She turned back to her original direction, her heart quivering, gut muscles contracting. There was no one there; at least no one visible. In this unlit jumble of fences and hedges and old boats it wouldn't have been hard to hide. She'd never been scared walking home before but something had changed now. She didn't understand what it was and she wasn't going to hang around trying to figure it out. Alice ran to her back door and didn't stop to breathe until it was bolted behind her.

PART TWO

10

UNSTABLE ISOTOPE

Frank stood alone on the empty road, wondering what to do. The punctured bicycle lay at his feet, its guilty front wheel still spinning from his kick. Bloody thing. He was a good five miles from the village, too far to walk, and yet there were no houses around, and no phone-boxes from where he could call Gail. Riding the bike on a flat tyre would surely only get him a few hundred yards before the tyre came slewing off the rim.

He pirouetted slowly, straining to see into the distance in every direction. But there was only desolation. On one side the dunes sat underneath a sky erased of all colour; inland, the setting sun had turned the wheat fields a pinky orange. A pair of swallows dipped then vanished.

Hell, there was nothing for it. He'd ride as far as he

could and if necessary dump the bike and walk the rest. Gail wouldn't care where he was. Doubtless she was sitting at Judy's patio table, getting sozzled, oblivious to Judy's need to bathe and bed the children *and* get dinner on before Maynard came home. Maynard wouldn't mind coming home to find Gail lounging about with her big sunglasses on and her tanned legs stretched out. Judy, Frank imagined, would feel torn between wanting this glamorous new friend and not wanting her husband so tempted.

He picked up the bike and rather gingerly pushed off. The wheel jarred on the asphalt, the vibrations going up through his wrists into his shoulders. Still, it was better than standing around moping.

Of course, Gail had snored for eight hours straight after the party, once he had dumped her on the bed in the spare room and removed her dress and shoes. He, on the other hand, had not been able to sleep and had walked around the house for an hour with all the lights blazing, talking himself up and down, letting the loops of thought play across his mind. At times he had felt beautifully detached from the whole situation, soaring above them all, not judging, only observing with a wry smile. He could hold himself apart from these people. His was a higher purpose. But then he had remembered Alice's bloody knee, and Judy's hand creeping up his own leg, and a sudden nausea made him bend over the kitchen sink. His reflection hung in the black window above it. Then the image of himself in the glass had begun to blur, from it shook loose the outline of another face. Faint and soft and yet clearly there. Composed of a million thrumming molecules and lifting itself from his own features. He had made a terrified whimpering sound. What the hell was happening to him? Was it his sight? Squeezed his eyes shut, and opening them again he had found the other face gone. Only his haggard reflection stared back at him.

The darkness had welcomed him. Outside in the garden, barefoot, he could breathe more easily. The air carried the scent of the sea, laced with grass and wildflowers. From the copse of trees across the meadow came the lazy drawl of an owl. Frank had stood where the two badgers had fought. For them – for all animals – there was none of this socialising, no futile bid to make yourself feel more alive by understanding others, by being loved by others. The necessities of life and the horror of death. That's all there could be for a badger.

The morning after the dinner party Gail had sat at their kitchen table in her underwear, ashen-faced and fat, chain-smoking. Her brokenness had made him consider telling her about Andrea, about seeing her in Maynard's house and the words she'd said to him. It sounded crazy; he knew that; and part of him wanted Gail to know. If he was going mad, why not share it around? Everyone could go crackers with him!

In the end, he had said nothing.

Only three hundred yards after he'd set off, a dilapidated wood and wire fence climbed out of the sand. It led to a path between the dunes, marked on one side by a continuation of the drunken fence posts, on the other by a chain of large painted pebbles. A cheerful variety of patterns and colours adorned the pebbles and some had rudimentary human forms daubed on them. Frank cast his eyes back and forth across this sight, confused. He'd ridden along this stretch of road before and hadn't noticed this path. With some effort he pushed his bike through the sand, then discovered a wide and substantial wooden plank half-buried in the centre of the path, making life a great deal easier. The corner of a building appeared.

Frank hesitated. He wasn't afraid, exactly. It was more that he felt a kind of foreboding. Until now the space and light of this coastline had belonged to him alone. It had been a refuge, somewhere for his thoughts to dissolve into the marshy air, the long horizon. Out here he felt that he could escape from what was pursuing him. He was disarmed by this place. What would he do if another claimed it as their own?

The shack had probably started life as a neat rectangle. Now, though, its many additions and repairs made it a rambling, scruffy mess. Driftwood, untreated timber, reclaimed doors had all been used, giving a patchwork effect, though every surface was much faded by the elements. It sat on a patch of ground sheltered on three sides by the dunes. Grey smoke wandered from a slim tin chimney.

'Hello,' Frank called out.

'Come round,' responded a female voice.

At the front of the shack was a broad wooden deck facing the sea. In the centre stood a gleaming motorbike, and crouching beside it a woman in dungarees, a red scarf knotted around her silver-grey hair. She stood up, screwdriver in hand, and cast an assessing look over him. Perhaps deciding Frank constituted no immediate threat to her safety she put the screwdriver down.

'Problem?' Her voice was deep and assertive.

'Puncture,' he said, feeling foolish to be stranded by such a trivial mechanical failure. 'I came out without a pump, and it's rather a long walk home.'

She raised her eyebrows and though her mouth remained straight, there was a glittering humour in her eyes. It was easy to see that she would have been a beautiful woman twenty years ago; indeed she was still handsome. Her face and bare arms were tanned and she was as tall as Frank, with strong shoulders, and though her stained dungarees and black boots were manly, they couldn't hide the heavy curves of her hips and breasts.

'Well that was a bit silly wasn't it? Besides you'll need more than a pump to fix a puncture. Come on, bring it over here. I enjoy rescuing damsels in distress. If I give you a spanner can you get the wheel out while I go and find my things? Oh, don't pull such a sour face. It's a lovely evening isn't it? No need to be so down in the dumps.'

God, he hadn't heard that expression for years, not since his mother was alive. It was one of her favourites.

Frank loosened the bolts on his front wheel and pulled it from the forks. From where he stood he could see little of what the woman was doing inside the shack – the interior was dim, there being only one small window to let in light. Just inside the door was a pile of driftwood pieces. Sand and sawdust were sent scurrying by the breeze.

'Here we are,' she said, coming back out with a handful of tools. 'Hand it over.'

Using two metal tyre levers she pulled the tyre from its rim, then peeled away the wounded inner tube.

'Are you at the power station now?' she asked as she pushed the pump onto the inner tube valve.

'Is it that obvious?'

She gave the pump a couple of strokes, just enough air

to generate a hissing from the hole. By holding the tube against the tyre she could trace the source of the puncture, embedded in the rubber. She prised it loose and held out a scored papery finger; on its tip lay a tiny white flint.

'There's the criminal in this little story,' she said, and when she looked up at him Frank was consumed by the intensity of being so close, so alone, with this stranger. She was, he guessed, about the same age his mother was when she died, but very different. Where his mother was feeble, this woman emitted a sense of strength and independence.

'Christ, I've seen bigger atoms.'

She laughed. 'What a preposterous thing to say. Come inside and we'll check the rest of the tube for leaks.'

The shack was one large room, apparently a jumble of home and artist's studio, for among the pieces of furniture, clothes, books and tin mugs were scattered pots of paintbrushes with stiff clean bristles, canvases blank or coloured, a stained apron and, standing to attention in the centre of the room, an easel. She – he wondered if he should know her name by now? – went to the back of the space, towards a metal sink. Next to it a two-ring gas burner held a saucepan roiling away. Frank felt obliged to say something, some piece of small-talk, to avoid an awkward silence. Christ, but what? What would Gail say in this situation?

'Sorry, were you just about to eat?'

She just waved away this comment.

'Have you lived here long?' he said.

'Too long, probably,' she replied, with her back to him as the sink filled up. Bloody artists. Ask a simple question...

'I'm Frank, by the way.'

'Come over here Frank, I'll show you how to check for punctures.'

'In the sink?'

'Oh gosh,' she exclaimed. 'You can turn plutonium into bombs but you can't mend a puncture.'

'I'm not making bombs. No one is making bombs here,' Frank said quickly, rather shocked at the accusation. All the same, he went and stood beside her, close enough to feel the heat radiating from her body, close enough to detect a sour trace of sweat, and he watched her plunge the black rubber tube into cold water then begin turning it slowly. Submerged, her fingers looked soft and pliable, like putty. When she dipped the site of the puncture under the water, a stream of bubbles fizzed out.

'Just that one. Now we can put a patch on it.'

They went outside and sat on the deck, she on the single chair there, he on an upturned bucket. He guessed she didn't get many visitors. Getting into the rhythm of a conversation, he found out a little more about her. How much she loved living so close to the sea, her daily routine of walking south along the beach, the fragments of foreign lives she found washed up there. The villagers left her alone. Once a week she went into the village so that she didn't forget the world of people, everything she'd left behind.

As she talked, she rubbed the inner tube with sandpaper, then applied glue to the area of the hole. When the sun had made the glue tacky she applied a rubber patch and stroked it into place.

'Only problem is, in this heat you might find the glue melts and the patch lifts. But it will get you home.'

As they waited for the glue to dry, she looked out to sea. Though the air was still warm, the silvery light dancing along the low waves gave an impression of coolness. A fishing boat was returning to harbour.

'What is it like inside that place, the power station?' she said, without turning to look at him.

'Inside? Pretty boring really. Laboratories, storage facilities, big pools for cooling. Nothing sinister. Everything is very carefully controlled.'

She reached down to the deck and picked up a pinch of sand, then tossed it into the air.

'It's everywhere though, isn't it? The radiation. In the sand, in the air, in the grass, on the pint glasses in The Anchor.' She was looking at him now, and he knew he wouldn't be able to continue to lie to her.

'I've had a beer in The Anchor,' he said. 'I'd say it benefits from a little uranium fizz.'

She laughed. 'You're like someone I used to know. He was a man of science too. Believed in progress, rational thought. Wanted to obliterate anything irrational, anything emotional. You can't approach life like that.'

'You don't believe in rational thought?'

'I no longer care to believe in anything. I've seen enough.'

'Is that why you're hiding out here?'

'You found me pretty easily didn't you? I'm not hiding from anything.'

She nodded at his scar. 'How did that happen?'

And before he knew what he was doing, the words were tumbling from his lips. 'I was cut by a woman named Andrea. She wanted revenge for what happened to her son. Her brother held me down while she used a kitchen knife on me. She was unhappy that I got off without going to prison. She knew strings had been pulled to get me off. On account of my work.'

She didn't ask the question he was expecting: what happened to Andrea's son?

'What happened to Andrea?'

'Sometimes I see her.'

'It's more common than you'd think, seeing things that aren't there. Being haunted doesn't make you so special. We all have our ghosts. Go on, go home to your wife.'

He hesitated, struggling to dam the words streaming into his mind.

'That's the first time I've said it. About what happened to me. I've never told anyone before. I always lie.'

'Then I must be special,' she said.

'What's your name?' he said.

'A name is like an old coat. When you're tired of it you can slip it off and throw it away.'

As Frank wheeled his repaired bicycle away from the shack, along the planks of wood, the wind blew sand through the spokes of his wheels, over his toecaps, over the painted pebbles. When he reached the road he turned around; the pebbles were almost completely submerged.

11

DECAY

Most of Frank's work took place around the reactor core, the centre of the whole operation, an area known colloquially as The Chambers. Here, time seemed to move at its own leisurely pace. There was no natural light and every system was maintained and monitored at the same steady level, day and night. Given the unspeakable power held in these quiet machines, every conversation between co-workers was weighted with the critical importance of getting it right. Not making mistakes. Mistakes and oversights were anathema. Here, at least according to the received truth, they could mean wholesale slaughter. Decimation of a largish chunk of British coastline. The ocean contaminated for generations. Within every room in the main reactor building a recorded sound played over the tannoy speakers, a repetitive thud not unlike a heartbeat. Day and night, that heart beat. One became inured to it, comforted by it. One's thoughts seemed to join its rhythm. If the heartbeat stopped, it meant there was an emergency that immediately endangered life. The local fire brigade would be coming hurtling along the coast road, its men struggling to pull on their protective suiting, every one of them afraid of the evil magic they were about to face.

One Thursday morning Frank was in the reactor core, extracting material for testing. Fully encased in a protective suit, with goggles sewn into the hood, his hands sweating inside heavy rubber gloves, he was working through a reinforced glass screen, using mechanical tools to grip the used fuel rods and lift them clear. Once he had what he wanted, he dropped the rods into a lead-lined box that could be pulled through a slot in the glass screen. Then a colleague sealed the box and placed it on a trolley to be taken to the lab.

Frank enjoyed this part of the job. On one hand, it felt like a child's game, something like hook-a-duck. On the other hand, he relished the pressure. Not that there was much chance of sparking an explosion or a fire, but a mistake would mean a team might have to be sent in to make a repair, and that was a stressful business. So the atmosphere in the room was hushed and serious. As he worked he could sense the two men waiting behind him, their soft breathing into filtered gas masks, their alertness, the stiff postures of their bodies.

It was two days since his encounter with the nameless woman on the beach. His memory of it was shaded, like a vivid dream that loses its colour as soon as the dreamer wakes. The whole thing had been unreal – the little shack, the way she spoke to him, the way he was physically drawn to her, magnetised even, though that sensation wasn't precisely sexual. She'd stirred something deep in him. He'd thought about her often since, and wanted to go back, wanted to give in to whatever force was being exerted upon him.

Plonk. There you go – five uranium fuel rods. Off to the lab for them, off for a cup of tea for Frank. He pulled off his face-mask, gloves, jacket and threw them in the dirty laundry bin and took a few careful steps over to the door. In theory everything on this side of the glass was clean, but experience had taught him that was a theory not to be trusted. Touch nothing and you had a higher chance of passing the door-check. At the door he raised his hand to the counter. Silence, and the little green light came on. Rather disappointed, he pushed the door open and unzipped his coverall.

The canteen was some distance from the reactor if you followed the official route – a yellow line painted on the tarmac of the service roads – but Maynard had shown him a shortcut that took you behind the health centre and the administration building, and came out in the delivery yard behind the canteen kitchens. After checking no one was around to see him, Frank ducked into the passageway beside the two huge back-up generators that looked to him like great hulking gorillas sitting on their haunches, pondering whether or not to rip this puny human's head off. An array of cigarette butts lined the side of the passage, along with the occasional mouse trap. The local wildlife knew no respect. They were drawn by the prospect of discarded food and would find a way into even the most secure building. The engineers were always pulling squashed or frazzled mice and squirrels out of machinery. Once, so the story went, an owl had somehow got into the reactor building and flown around in panicked circles, crawing and crying, while all the staff stood around dumbfounded. Eventually someone remembered that one of the maintenance men was an amateur falconer, and he found his security clearance suddenly upgraded so that he could get in and rescue the bird.

Frank turned a corner and saw, fifty yards ahead, a man and a woman standing close together. Maynard, in his blue overalls and white hard hat. And facing him, so small and slender in her white uniform, with her hair tied back, and her face upturned to his, was Alice. They both turned to Frank, yet neither showed any kind of surprise or dismay. Indeed, Alice's smile faded only a little when she recognised Frank. It became not the smile of someone she was pleased to see, but rather the smile of someone who liked being caught doing something she shouldn't. Maynard was probably trying to maintain a straight face while his oafish brain scrambled to find something vaguely credible to say.

'Hello you two. Taking a break?' said Frank. Alice shuffled away from Maynard.

'Young Alice here was just asking me about the pros and cons of marriage,' said Maynard. At this, young Alice raised her eyebrows and shook her head.

'Why, has Anthony popped the question?'

'No, he hasn't, and he doesn't need to,' she said. 'I don't need a ring on my finger.'

'Or a ball and chain on your ankle, eh?' said Maynard.

She looked up at him, then back to Frank.

'Your friend has some rather retrogressive ideas, doesn't he?' she said.

He's not my friend, Frank wanted to say. He felt like she was trying to ease him into saying something like this – something provocative that might anger Maynard.

Maynard came over to Frank and gave him a hearty slap between the collarbones. Then he laid his hand on Frank's shoulder and squeezed, uncomfortably hard.

'I think you'll find all men are pretty simple beasts really, when it comes down to it, eh Frank?'

Unseen by Alice, Maynard's thumb was digging into Frank's muscle. That fucker. He won't get a rise out of me, though, not now. Not in front of her. I'm in control of this situation.

'I couldn't agree more,' said Frank. 'We only want one thing.'

Alice folded her arms. 'And what's that then?'

'A nice cup of tea,' said Frank, and even Maynard laughed at that one.

Ducking out of the other man's grip, Frank stepped past Alice, giving her only the briefest glance. And as he strode on towards the canteen he heard her giggle.

12

ALPHA

Gripping his tray, Frank shuffled past the glistening sausages with burnt ends, fried eggs bathing in yellow oil and clumps of soggy chips. Behind the food, women in stained white coats brandished huge metal spoons as totems of their ultimate authority, dishing out their produce to scientists in spotless white tunics.

In front of him was a great hulk of an engineer in green overalls. And behind Frank was one of the women who worked in the offices, chattering with a friend about some disastrous love affair. She was standing close to Frank – her tray kept nudging the small of his back – close enough for him to smell her sickening perfume above the food.

The woman laughed and he felt her lean into his ear.

What does he think, eh?

Frank froze.

Does that silly man think you'll go running to his wife, tell her that her husband has been flirting with little girls? Or do the same to her boyfriend? How ridiculous. How pointless that would be. No, he can trust us with his secret, can't he?

Frank spun round, sending his glass of milk toppling. The white liquid sloshed across his tray and onto the floor by the feet of the woman, who was still talking to her friend.

'Watch it!' she said, drawing back from him with a look of alarm and disgust.

'You weren't talking to me... No, nothing, sorry,' Frank mumbled.

'I *am* talking to you – I'm saying watch it. I only got these shoes last week. Go and get a cloth from Brenda. Jesus.'

• • •

Over the next few days, simply by saying nothing, Frank demonstrated his complicity to Maynard, and Maynard's attitude became warmer. Now I really am one of the lads, Frank told himself – with all the privileges that confers. Adultery, cover-ups, coarse jokes and testosterone-charged nonsense. Excellent.

He even got invited to the pub.

In the Anchor both bars were busy with fishermen straight off the boats, so the three scientists stood in a huddle in the saloon bar, by the redundant fireplace. It was a homely place, with the same sort of array of unexplained photographs framed on the walls that one usually found in pubs, a stone floor covered by a couple of tatty rugs that would have stunk of fish had the landlord's wife not made the fishermen remove their boots at the door, and cheap furniture that creaked whenever you shifted your weight. The windows gave a grubby view of the sea, though of course no one was very interested in that.

Frank had learnt over the past few weeks that the fishermen tended to be a morose lot. From what he could understand of their strange, soft language, they liked to bemoan the authorities, the weather, Dutch trawlers making incursions and, most of all, their wives. The most penetrating hardship of being at sea seemed to be coming home. There were other pubs in the village, and many of the power station workers drank at The King's Head, which was also frequented by the farming crowd, but Frank quite liked The Anchor. Apart from its scenic position on the harbour, he enjoyed watching the fishermen, their sun-hatched faces and animal eyes. It was such an elemental, primitive way to make a living. A world away from what he did, and yet only a few miles of water separated them as they all worked. The power station depended on the sea for its cooling systems, and as a convenient place to dispose of waste.

'So, come on then young Anthony, what are your intentions regarding the delightful Alice?' asked Maynard.

Anthony laughed at him. 'My intentions? Christ, what are you, her Victorian grandfather?'

Maynard smiled, but it was obviously forced. Any reference to his age irked him.

'She thinks you're going to rescue her from this place, from marrying one of this lot,' Maynard said, gesturing at the drinkers around them.

'Marry? Steady on. Plenty of time for that.'

Anthony looked shocked at the suggestion, and failed to ask the obvious question of how Maynard knew of Alice's ambitions. Frank remembered the look on her face, that moment before they'd heard him approaching along the passage, the cleverness, the feigned supplication to Maynard's masterly ways. Frank felt the temperature of his anger rising. Was he jealous? No. It was true that he did often feel pangs of envy when he encountered men who could so confidently and brazenly seduce women. That what for him had always been an agonising and usually inept business could be second nature to other men seemed brutally unfair. But no, he didn't feel jealous of Maynard in any way. Indeed he pitied him. He was an animal, forever bound to his low urges.

If anything, perversely, Frank was jealous on behalf of Gail; was Maynard already bored of her? No, that wasn't how men like him operated. They cast their nets wide, seeing who might bite, then went in for the kill. Any good-looking woman would receive their attention.

Gail could look after herself. Alice could not.

'Marry her, get her pregnant, get the hell out of here. Soon as you can, I'd say,' said Frank loudly.

'How many have you had?' said Maynard.

Anthony frowned. 'But her family are all here.'

'Precisely,' replied Frank with a triumphant laugh. 'Who doesn't want to escape their family? That girl has got potential, you mark my words, but you've got to let her breathe, let her escape this place. She'll suffocate here.'

'Frank, keep your voice down, for Christ's sake,' said Maynard.

Frank, however, was feeling the liberation afforded

by three pints of strong beer. He had people on his side, pushing him along – Gail, the woman on the beach, even Andrea was with him now. They were at his shoulder, whispering encouragement. He would be a new kind of man. Honourable, yet not afraid to do what was necessary. He could protect Alice by persuading Anthony to take her away.

'Well, she's just a local girl, mate,' said Anthony, looking crestfallen at the sudden responsibility being placed on him. 'Just a bit of fun, you know?'

'Just a local yokel eh? Good for a quick fuck?'

Two men standing nearby turned and glared at Frank, who grinned maniacally back at them.

Maynard was making strange hissing noises that Frank did not understand. He and Anthony were as pitiful as each other.

Frank raised his glass high into the air and called out, 'Gentlemen! A toast. To girls with webbed feet.'

The pub went quiet.

Fifty pairs of eyes turned on Frank. Then a bottle came sailing through the air, describing a lazy spinning arc before clattering against the door frame, missing Frank's head by an inch.

'Get out,' called someone.

'Get out, you're not welcome,' came another cry. Frank noticed the landlord reaching for the cricket bat that lay conspicuously behind the bar.

Nearer to them stood a lean young man who was wearing a woollen hat, despite the heat, and appeared to have broken his nose in the past. He jabbed a finger at each of the three scientists.

'You heard the man. We don't want you here, do you

understand?' he said.

Despite having Maynard's restraining paw on his arm, Frank took a step towards the young man. He felt energy, pure and unstoppable, as if huge electric currents were rushing up his back and into his shoulders.

'But my dear chap, don't *you* understand? We'll be here long after you've all gone. We are the future. You'll all be out of jobs, the sea will be barren and dead. And your children will be working for us.'

This forecast so flummoxed the young fisherman that he could neither respond, nor find the wherewithal to throw a punch. But the anger burned in his eyes and Frank fed on that. Inside him, buried deep, there was something like a dark core; he usually pictured it as a hole, small and black, and now charged with radiation. Growing, gnawing, hungry to expand. It needed fury.

Acid filled his mouth. His fingernails dug into his palms.

Finally, the young man thought of a reply. 'Oh yeah... and what you going to eat with your chips? Fucking pluto-whateveryoucallit?'

This got a belly laugh from his peers, and the tension of the previous moment ebbed away, disappointing a man sitting at the bar, so fat that the stool had disappeared beneath him, who in a gruff voice now encouraged his colleagues to 'Teach the arrogant cunt a lesson.'

Frank picked up his pint glass from the narrow shelf where he'd placed it, swung his arm back and launched it – half-full – over the crowd. He did this so swiftly that no one had the chance to duck or dodge. Beer sprayed into the faces of those nearest to him while the glass flew to its target, smacking the fat man on the side of the head. After the glass had bounced to the floor, the man's head crashed onto the bar, then, ever-so-slowly, his bulk slid off the bar stool, bumping the unconscious head down with it.

In the next fraction of a second, before the roar that was to erupt from the drinkers around them, before the landlord could get out from behind the bar, Frank found himself outside. An explosion of light, the release of sprinting across the cobbles, giddy with joy, laughing hysterically. The herd of lumbering beasts might be gathering behind the fleeing men, but it was too dumb to catch them.

Tearing out of the village in Maynard's car, leaving their pursuers yelling in the street, Anthony began laughing like a lunatic. Frank reached back to the back seat where Anthony was sprawled, and shook his hand. Maynard, however, was silent and grim-faced. One of the fishermen had managed to plant a good kick into the side of his car as he struggled to get it into gear.

'Christ, Frank,' giggled Anthony. 'That bloke at the bar was out cold. You're crazy. One thing's for sure. We won't be going in that pub again for a while.'

On the outskirts of the village, as the road dived into the marshes behind the sand dunes, Maynard slammed on the brakes.

'Get the fuck out of my car,' he said, his voice quiet but underscored by rage.

'What?' said Frank.

'Get out,' Maynard roared.

Frank didn't move, so Maynard himself got out, marched around the bonnet, opened the passenger door and grabbed Frank's arm. He yanked hard and Frank toppled sideways, his hands scraping through the gravel on the roadside before his body crumpled. Being drunk, he felt no pain from his landing. Just a confused swirling sense of injustice.

'Oh boy,' he croaked, as he clambered to his feet. 'You are making a serious...mistake... You are making...'

Maynard's hand flew up to Frank's throat and fastened around it. That same thumb that had dug into his shoulder only the day before, now pressed Frank's windpipe.

'Shut up, just shut up you fucking lunatic. I know how you got that scar. How you blow up when you lose your temper. But I'm not as fucking impressed as your wife clearly is. I've seen your sort before. You don't scare me. You're just one of those little weird ones who never joined in at school. Too busy wanking behind the bike sheds. You just need to keep your mouth shut and not cause me trouble, do you understand?'

Before Frank could reply – and he intended to do so civilly – Maynard brought his head forward in a swift motion to headbutt him. Not a full-blooded blow, more of a tap, but the surprise sent Frank tottering backwards. His feet caught underneath him and he fell into the grass verge. From there he watched Maynard accelerate away.

Silence. Blasted silence.

Through the gloaming he walked, surrounded by the murderous wildlife, dragged forward by the hum and glow of the power station in the distance. The sea pushing at the shore, relentless, the sky of scraped charcoal and open to any possibility. Anything could happen now. He was free to act. This was the best thing to happen to him since Karen had got herself knocked up by that little sod. There was anger in Frank's blood, yes, but his mind was cool and rational. Maynard had taken off the mask and underneath he was monstrous.

• • •

Here was his reward. Standing in the doorway, wearing only her nightie, the curves of her body just discernible in the silvery light. The house was dark, silent, warm. Frank sat in the armchair with his hands on his thighs. He'd been there some time, waiting for the night to calm him down. When he first got in, his head was pounding, his scraped palms beginning to sting, and his throat was parched. Yet he'd ignored all that and instead stood at the window of the front room with the curtains open, staring across the road at Maynard's house. The car was on the drive, the lights were all off. Maynard was there lying beside Judy. Thinking, no doubt, of Alice. Probably having a quiet wank. The cunt.

'What have you got to tell me?' said Gail in a sleepy voice. 'What have you boys been up to?'

'Your admirer doesn't like me,' he said, after a long silence.

'I'm surprised you care.'

'He's a coward,' Frank said. 'And of course I care, I'm a very sensitive person.'

She laughed. 'I know you are darling, you just hide it so well. Why don't you come to bed?'

For every action there is an equal and opposite reaction. Newton's Third Law. True in physics, true in life. If you sin, you will be punished. It was one of the undeniable rhythms to life. And if you are the one delivering the punishment, you will be rewarded.

'I like it here,' he said. 'Come here and let me tell you something.'

She walked across the room. Hitching up her nightie, she straddled him and bent forward so that her mouth nuzzled beneath his ear. Inhaling the luxurious musk of her body, he whispered to her.

'I think this place will be good for me. I'm stronger here. I see things more clearly.'

'Let me help you,' she breathed, and slipped her finger into the buckle of his belt.

• • •

Later, lying in bed, she listened to his teeth grinding against each other. It was one of those noises that were barely audible, yet once you heard it you could hear nothing else. It was the sound of that machine mind of his, still whirring. No, actually it was deeper than that. It was his subconscious crashing through into his body. He was curled foetal-like, facing away from her, and his spine, shoulders were tense. Occasionally his legs burst into a spasm kick then his knees came back up.

After they'd finished, in the living room, she had gingerly climbed off him and lain on her back on the carpet with her legs in the air, one hand under the small of her back – give the swimmers every chance of making it upstream.

Frank didn't move from the armchair. He just sat there with his cock softening, lolling, trousers around his ankles, and a look of bewilderment on his face. She laughed, too loud and nervous, and his expression darkened. He stood up, but he was staring across the room at the door, as if seeing someone else there. His eyes were wild. Suddenly afraid, she snatched up her clothes and ran through the empty doorway.

He said he wanted a baby but it was lip service, to keep her happy. He didn't have the first idea about what life would be like with children.

Well, if he couldn't give her a baby, perhaps another man could. This gnawing hunger for a child was surely going to send her crazy if she couldn't satisfy it. She'd always fantasised about other men – it was a kind of habit from her teenage years – but recently they were all fathers. Family men who were probably bored of their wives and their once-a-month sex lives. All of whom could get her pregnant quicker than her radioactive husband. Jesus it was so unfair.

Oh God, what was she saying?

Turning away from her husband, she began to cry softly into the pillow. He was slipping away from her. He was nervy, quick to temper. And sometimes he seemed frightened when he had no obvious cause to be so, yet when she questioned him he clammed up. So much for their fresh start. She'd never been scared of Frank before – not even after the incident at Barton Hall – but now she was afraid of his volatility. Something – or someone – was changing him, and she felt powerless to stop it. They'd come to this place to escape the demons of their recent past, and yet here, something far worse was consuming him.

• • •

Deep blackness. Foxes screeching outside. Gail asleep beside him, rasping a little, lying on her back. The air in the bedroom thick with sex and sweat and dirt.

A whimpering sound, but from where? Inside the house. In the living room, the hallway? Frank held his breath and tried to tune out Gail. A human sound, but also like a wounded animal. As if filled with acid, Frank's stomach burned. And as he swung them out of bed, his legs felt like dead wood, ready to crumble under the slightest pressure.

He was naked. Clothes – both his and Gail's – lay crumpled on the floor around the bed, and in the darkness it was impossible to tell whose was whose. Besides, he didn't need clothes. He stepped through the bedroom door and shut it behind him.

In the hallway, close to the front door, was a body. It made another sound but did not move. From where he stood it was hard to see anything more than the outline. From the tone of the sounds he guessed it was a woman. His toes moved through the soft carpet.

Now he saw a bare foot, tiny, almost childlike. A pair of legs in shapeless trousers. Dark hair tied back. Gaunt face mottled black and white, eyes swollen and shut, teeth bared against the pain.

'What have they done to you?' he whispered. She didn't respond, so he squatted beside her and put his mouth close to her ear. The stench of her poured down his throat. 'Andrea, what have they done to you?'

One eye cracked open. Just a glimmer of life, and yet he felt shamed by her power.

Will you really let him get away with that? Are you so weak? So lily-livered?

Look what they've done to me, those bitches. They're nothing but animals. And I'm inside because of you, don't you forget that. Don't you forget that, little man.

With a groan she shifted position, sitting up and resting on her elbow. Now, in the moonlight filtering through the frosted window of the front door he could better see her injuries.

She reached out a white claw and grabbed his balls. Held them snug in her palm, and as she pressed a smile spread across her bloodied lips.

Now I've got you, haven't I?

13

BETA

Never an early riser, Gail was still in bed, half-asleep, when she heard Frank leaving the house. So, no goodbye kiss, no whispered affections. Not that all that meant much; she knew that in the mornings he often woke with some complicated work problem on his mind, the kind of horribly intricate calculation that to her was as alien as a message from deepest space. Once his head had filled with such a puzzle there was no space left for anything as trivial as marital intimacy. She wondered if Maynard was the same, whether Judy suffered the same neglect. It was clear Judy thought she and Gail were kin. They were in it together, the wives of Atomics.

Gail took a bath and stared for too long at her empty belly. Then dressed, had some tea and toast, and drove into the village. Since walking away from the school gates that hot morning two weeks before, she'd been existing in a strange languorous state. Days passed slowly, but not miserably. The weather was still glorious, allowing for stretches of sunbathing and beach-combing. Judy was around in the afternoons for an early gin. Sometimes Gail went for a drive around the neighbouring villages looking for cottages for sale (there was no way on God's earth she was going to bring up a child in that bloody bungalow). In a place called Rotherfield she found a pub on the village green selling bacon butties and local cider. When baby comes next spring, she told herself, we'll come here and play on the grass, lunch, watch out for daffodils.

It couldn't last, this hiatus in her life. The weather would break, she'd get bored, but until then... Anyway, surely she would fall pregnant soon. And then the work would start – on moving house, on the nursery, buying all the things a baby needs, on preparing Frank...

After parking just off the high street, she visited the ramshackle book shop and the newsagents at the northern end of town, then walked the length of the high street, which ran parallel to the sea defences, gazing idly into shop windows, smiling hello at those who greeted her as they passed. Tuesday morning and there were housewives out to replenish their kitchens, mothers with prams, old ladies in beige raincoats.

Though to any of these observers her movement would have appeared casual, and she could almost convince herself of its aimlessness, she was in fact being drawn towards a very specific destination.

The doctor's surgery was a modern building at the far end of town. Beyond it only a few tumbledown fishing huts and the rather shabby yacht club. Hexagonal in shape, with a flat roof and expansive windows that seemed to wobble under the sun's glare, the surgery had been paid for by the Authority as part of their attempts to mollify the local community. An unfortunate strategy, Maynard had told them over dinner (before events had unravelled in such a hilarious fashion), because some of the less bright locals imagined the construction of a new doctor's surgery to be a tacit admission that the power station would make everyone sick.

Across the street, Gail paused. There was nothing wrong with her. At least, she wasn't ill. And yet the building had some kind of magnetic power over her. She wanted to go inside and tell someone everything. More than that, she wanted someone to tell her that it was going to be all right, that a baby would come eventually, that there was nothing wrong with her. And in time she would come out of those doors with the happy news confirmed, congratulations ringing behind her, the future opening like the sea's horizon.

Again she felt on the brink of tears. God, what a fucking wreck! Wasn't it supposed to be the rampant hormones *after* you fell pregnant that turned you a bit nutty?

She wasn't going in. Not now. What could they tell her that she didn't already know?

She turned away and a moment later heard her name being called.

'Gail!' A clear, confident voice.

A young woman in white scrubs strode down the path from the surgery doors. Her dark hair was pulled back into a tight ponytail and her pale face bore no make-up. Alice looked so different it took Gail several seconds to recognise her.

Gail was stunned that the smiling girl was apparently so keen to talk to her. She really didn't want to talk to anyone right at that moment but it was unavoidable now.

She blinked back the tears that had been about to come, pushed her shoulders back and fixed a smile. Alice called out a breezy hello and stepped across the road. In flat shoes she seemed smaller than Gail remembered. The white uniform lent a sense of the surreal, as if she was an otherworldly being.

'Are you going in?' Alice asked.

'No, no, I was just...exploring. I haven't been this far before, and Judy mentioned the surgery was up here.'

'I was just getting my coil fitted,' Alice said. 'Well, I suppose you'll need to come here soon enough.'

'What do you mean?'

'Well, for the baby. You know, when it happens for you.' Alice was still smiling, though her eyes now were uncertain.

God was it that obvious? Or had she said something at Judy's house the other night while drunk? Probably both.

Alice shook two cigarettes out of a pack and gave one to Gail. They stood close together to light them, struggling with a box of matches and the sea wind.

'I heard the old boy in there is a bit too friendly at times,' Gail said. Without speaking they turned to walk into town, falling comfortably into step.

'Ratcliffe? I've heard the same but he doesn't dare touch me, he knows what he'd get back. My brother's well-known around the village. He's a great useless lump most of the time but he does a good line in threatening behaviour, if you know what I mean. Besides, there's another doctor; younger – he's all right. Ask for him, he'll look after your baby.'

It was strange and reassuring to hear this young woman speak of Gail's baby as if it was a real thing, an event that would definitely happen. Of course Alice was naïve. Doubt and fear had yet to creep into her mind, her body was capable and robust. To her anything was possible. Gail missed feeling like that.

Alice said, 'Do you think I should apologise to Judy for the other night? I mean it got a bit out of control at the end didn't it?'

'No, I think it's Maynard who needs to apologise, don't you? I mean, if you were to apologise, that's an admission of guilt. And I'd say it was Maynard who was misbehaving, right?'

'I suppose so. Well, he was trying to, wasn't he? Your husband was very brave.'

'Brave? Crazy, more like it. I don't know what gets into his head. I mean, it's not like you were in any danger were you?'

Alice didn't reply and Gail wondered if she was disappointed. Had she expected of Gail a more electrified response? Some outrage? What Gail really wanted to say was, older men want to fuck younger women. A boring fact of life. Usually, though, they waited until their wife wasn't around.

'What do you think of him? Maynard, I mean,' Alice said after a long pause. Gail took a breath. She didn't want to get into a conversation about boys with a girl like this. She was too old, too tired. And yet...there was something attractive in this girl's manner. It was in the buoyancy of her step and a hint of humour in her voice, as if whatever she said, none of it was really worth worrying about too much.

'You mean, do I think he's dishy?'

Alice giggled at the word. 'In the novel I'm reading at the moment one of the girly characters would probably call him beastly, then throw herself at him.'

The novel, Gail noted. She knew what Alice was saying: I'm no ordinary bumpkin. I'm getting out of here.

'Perhaps that's what Judy did,' Gail said. 'I can imagine her saying beastly.'

Grinning, Alice slipped her arm into Gail's and nudged a little closer. 'I just knew we were going to be friends,' she said.

They walked a little way in silence. Gail told herself to give the girl a chance, not to push her away.

'I used to be like you,' she said. 'Carefree, I suppose you'd call it.'

'You're not that much older than me.'

'Women get old faster than men, you know.'

Alice turned to her, frowning. 'Eh?'

'The ticking clock? Make the most of your freedom; that's what I'd say to you.'

'Are you friends with Judy and Maynard?' Alice said.

'Friends? We're neighbours. We've only been here a few weeks.' How long had they been in Setonisle? Gail had no idea. 'But I like Judy, yes.'

'And Maynard?'

'Alice, Maynard is not the sort of man who has female friends. Maynard is the sort of man who has a binary way of looking at women. Either he'd like to fuck you, or he wouldn't.' And, Gail thought, we both fall into the former category.

14

GAMMA

The two men stood facing each other in the street, each holding a full bin bag. Maynard looked tired. His red-rimmed eyes struggled to hold Frank's unwavering gaze.

'Listen…' Maynard started, shifting his weight to compensate for the bag. 'I'm sorry about the other night. All right? I was out of order.'

Frank said nothing, then turned and walked over to his dustbin, dropped his bag in, then returned to face Maynard. Might as well enjoy the moment, he told himself.

He's not sorry.

'You're sorry?'

The muscles around Maynard's jaw tensed. Now he could only nod his reply.

Just pretend. You need to keep close to him, keep your enemies close, Frank. You need to know what he's doing to that girl.

A bright smile spread across Frank's face. 'Forget it, and I'm sorry too. It was just a crazy night, wasn't it?'

Maynard laughed in relief. 'I'm getting too old for that sort of thing. Right, well I better get to work. See you at lunchtime?'

Over the next few days Frank felt listless and tired. He wasn't ill – at least he had no obvious symptoms – and yet the smallest task felt a struggle. In sympathy, it seemed, the summer also lost its vigour. The sky turned white. The sun became just an ache on the edge of one's vision. And as the heat ebbed, the land looked crumpled and withered. Gail told him to take a couple of days off work, to sit in the garden and recover. It was the pressure of the move and the new job, she said. Inevitable that it would catch up with him. But Frank didn't want to dodge work. Indeed it was the only thing he looked forward to because it offered him chances, slim though they were, of more contamination.

He knew he was feeling terrible because he wasn't getting enough radiation. If he wanted to feel strong again, to have that same energy as when he had pummelled that stupid boy, he would have to replenish his supply. Top himself up, as it were.

Getting contaminated was easy; doing so without being noticed less so. The staff at the health clinic kept a log of everyone sent their way, and the security people kept their own log of accidents, spillages and leaks. Both logs were, according to Maynard, lengthy. No one bothered to analyse them, nor share them with the Authority. All the same, anything unusual or repetitive would ring the proverbial alarm bells. Someone would notice a name that popped up regularly.

Frank decided to stage one or two minor accidents to get himself a half-decent dose. Then, if the opportunity arose, he might create some bigger event – something that would really give him the fuel he needed. All of this he would do alone.

His opportunity came when, working in the reactor core, extracting fuel rods for analysis, he noticed a loose pile casing. He only had one other worker with him in the room, so it was easy to send him off to fetch a tool, while Frank spun the screws so loose that as soon as he tried to pull the rod through into its lead box, the whole thing fell apart.

'My God,' said Bob, his voice growing hysterical. 'Fuck, this is... We need to shut this down, get out of here. We've got to get out of here.'

Frank gave him a shove on the shoulder. 'Shut up you idiot. Calm down. There's no danger. You don't understand anything do you?'

Fifteen minutes later Frank was lying on a bed in the health clinic with Alice looking down at him. Bob was in the shower, no doubt scrubbing as if his life depended on it. It was unsettling to be here alone with Alice (her colleague, the formidable Beryl, was in the next room painting her nails). The concern in her eyes made her look so naïve. Bless her, Gail would have said.

'That was a high dose,' Alice said.

'I feel fine. Never better,' he replied, though in truth he did feel a little queasy.

'It will be reported to old Parker. You know that?'

Old Parker. Frank had forgotten about him. Perhaps there would be a summons, an interview. The thought crossed Frank's mind that if Parker was looking for a way to get rid of him, this kind of thing might give him an excuse. If necessary Frank could blame Bob; the poor bugger would probably be happy to take early retirement. As Alice wrote in her logbook, Frank tried to conjure the question he really wanted to ask her, but it was hard to put it in a way that wouldn't offend her.

'Has Maynard been here?' he said.

'No. Why? Has he had a dose?'

'Not that I know of. But he'd probably give himself a dose on purpose just to see you.'

A smile flickered on her face, quickly suppressed.

'That would be silly.'

Frank grabbed her wrist and held her. She winced and glared at him. 'Just be careful,' he said, then let go.

'You're the loopy one,' she shot back. 'Not Maynard. He's harmless.'

Frank shook his head. 'Don't be so sure. He's got bad intentions.'

'I don't know what you're going on about.'

'If you need help, tell me. I'll look after you. I will.'

She turned away, rubbing her wrist. 'Go and get in the shower. And make sure to wash between your ears. God knows, that stuff is sending you over the edge.'

• • •

The sea was flat and grey. A little way out an oily patch picked up the hazy afternoon sunshine. They sat on the edge of her wooden deck with a pot of tea and two mugs between them. She wore stout sandals on her brown feet, Frank pushed his white toes into the sand, and the sensation brought back a memory of family holidays in Devon. Of his mother digging deep holes for him to jump into, and his father asleep on a deckchair, a newspaper across his face. He'd always treasured those endless summer days on the beach because Mum seemed so happy, so alive. It was as if being out in the elements, wrapped in the wind and the sun, somehow gave her an electric charge, revived her from the dull stupors she was otherwise prone to sink into. An unfortunate image really, given the electric shock therapy she was put through later.

'Shall I be mother?'

She poured the tea. She'd offered him a beer but alcohol was the last thing he fancied. For the last day or so he'd been feeling sick, to the point of barely eating anything other than some dry toast. Even the prospect of spreading some butter on it had turned his stomach. And last night he'd woken up in the small hours with a pounding headache. With Gail snoring gently beside him, he'd lain very still, limbs spread, palms flat on the sheet, and tried to focus on each part of his body in turn. He was, he knew, a man who lived in his head. The physical world was always there of course, but only intermittently did he actually stop to sense it, with the result that when he did, it stirred him deeply. The freezing North Sea water around his naked body, the ache in his legs on a long bike ride, pushing his toes into this sand. And what he felt, lying there in bed, were the electrons buzzing about inside him, abrasive and ruthless, stripping away the old Frank, the man who cared what other people thought of him, the man who watched but was too cowardly to act.

Yes, there would be some side-effects, but the net gain was enormous.

'She wanted revenge?' she said.

He nodded.

'For her son? For what you did to him?'

'Yes.'

'Understandable isn't it? If you had a child and he was hurt by someone, you'd have the same thoughts wouldn't you?'

'Having the thoughts is different to actually doing something,' Frank said, looking sideways at her profile. Her shrewd eyes were gazing out to sea. 'She planned it carefully. Made sure I was alone, that there was nowhere for me to go. It was calculated. She knew precisely what she wanted to do to me.'

'Is that worse than what you did to her son?'

'I see her sometimes, or at least I think I do. Then she vanishes.'

'I know. But I asked you about what you did to her son. How long was he in hospital? Do you think he's haunted by visions of you?'

Such a thought had occurred to Frank before. Indeed, in the first few days after he'd been released from hospital himself, Gail had told him that the boy's physical injuries would heal, given time, but the mind was another matter. You're his devil now, she'd said. You'll both be scarred for life.

'Why did you do it?'

'Revenge.'

'For what?'

'He, Jonny was his name, beat his girl up. In her own front room, while her parents were out, left her with two black eyes, bruises everywhere, a fractured rib. She was petrified of him, and afterwards she wouldn't leave the house. Made herself a prisoner. She worked with me at Barton Hall, but then she had to leave.'

'So you took revenge on her behalf? You were angry?'

'I was looking for an opportunity. I hated that boy more than I've ever hated anything in my entire life. I wanted to destroy him.'

'Sounds like you came pretty close.'

'I might have killed him.'

'If someone hadn't pulled you off?'

Frank didn't respond. A seagull had landed a few feet in front of them and was stalking about in a circle with a desperate, agitated look. Its glassy eyes were baleful. Fucking humans, it seemed to be thinking. That evening in the Coach and Horses in Wallingford Frank had let the anger surge out of him. For so long that anger had been wound tightly through his body like a long worm, squeezing and squeezing, sucking all his energy.

The policeman who arrested him understood. He wasn't a big man, but he was wiry and twitchy. He did everything fast. His handwriting, as he took down a statement, was atrocious. 'He provoked you, didn't he sir? He insulted you?' Not understanding, Frank at first shook his head. So the policeman laid down his pen. Looked him in the eye.

'You got angry, right? You didn't stop soon enough. It happens. He's a little oik. You're a professional man. You're no pub brawler. He must have provoked you.' Now comprehending, Frank nodded, and felt the soft protection of conspiracy close over his head.

No such cover-up for Andrea, of course. For knifing him

she got six months in Holloway. What a sorry little storm they'd all created. Jonny's face permanently rearranged, Karen refusing to leave the house for fear of bumping into him, Andrea in prison, and in Oxford, Frank lying in a hospital bed with more face bandages than the elephant man.

'Why did you feel so angry about her, about this girl in particular? I mean, it's horrible, but it's common enough, and you had no special relationship with her did you?'

'She was just a nice girl,' he said, aware of how ludicrous that sounded. 'And...well, for a while I'd been feeling...I don't know, maybe anonymous. Invisible, even.'

'Do you still feel like that? Invisible?' she said, still looking out to sea. This conversation was a great deal easier if they didn't look at each other. Her questions seemed detached from her, more like echoes from the caverns of his own mind.

'No, I want to rescue something.'

'Rescue something? What? Love? Your wife has stood beside you hasn't she? A great deal of women would have left you by now. Actually I was hoping you might want to carry on destroying things. That's much more interesting to me. Don't mistake me for a kindly old woman who wants you to be a good boy.'

Now he looked at her, surprised, and she turned to look back at him. Behind her glimmering blue eyes he felt the power that he wanted. Whatever pain had driven her to hide herself away here on the beach for all these years, was now transmuting into an intensity that was pouring out of her and into him. Not blinking, not moving, they stared into each other's eyes for minutes, days, years. Her will was undeniable.

He saw that violence was attractive to her. Just like Parker, she relished its energy, its youth. She was drawn to the danger.

Eventually he saw that her lips were moving.

'...to me. Have you heard the story of the wild man who once lived in these parts? No, I didn't think so. Well, this was a long time ago of course, seven hundred years or thereabouts. The story goes that a fisherman caught him in his nets, out beyond Lumb Bank. He was only a little man, if that's what you could call him – less than five feet tall, and covered all over in scales, with fur on his hands and face. And he had a fishtail. An ugly thing he was, coarse and wild, and strong too – when they got ashore it took four good men to hold him down. He wailed and gnashed and spat in their faces but they held him until the army came. He was chained up in the dungeon down at Orford but the chains couldn't hold him. One morning he simply vanished. Most folks assumed he'd gone back to the sea, and that wasn't such a bad thing. If he came from the sea, he should be allowed to live there.

'Anyway some time passed, and then people began reporting sightings of the wild man again. It was said that he could be seen in the marshes after dark. Having learnt his lesson about men, he was careful to stay hidden, but just occasionally he came near a farm or lonely cottage and was seen. Over the weeks and months he became bolder and the locals left him to roam as he pleased. They hated the lord whose castle he'd been chained up in, so no one was going to betray the merman.'

She paused to take a sip of tea. Before continuing with her tale, for a moment she held Frank's eyes, daring him to scoff. He did not. It was a long time since someone had told him a story.

'They began to leave food out for him. He built a shelter down among the sand dunes, and some of the braver villagers visited him there. He was gruff and smelly and his talking was rudimentary but over time he learnt more words, which he supplemented with his own kind of sign language. It was said that the wild man had magical powers, that he could see deep into a man's heart and know that man's true desires. Not a fortune-teller or any of that hocus pocus. He simply told you the truth inside your soul. If you were a black-hearted murderer, or wanted to be but hadn't yet given in to your urges, he would tell you. If you were due to marry a pretty girl, but deep down you loved her ugly sister, he would tell you. If you wanted to fuck a goat, he would tell you. He passed no judgment on whether that was right or wrong because he had no sense of morality.'

Frank raised his eyebrows. 'The people round here must have lived in chaos, if everyone gave in to their deepest desires.'

She shrugged. 'Perhaps. Or perhaps they learned how to withstand the chaos, how not to give in to themselves. If so, they could be said not to be deceiving themselves. As you are now.'

'Me?'

'Think of me as the merman,' she said.

'You're much more attractive than he sounds.'

'I can see how lonely you are.'

Frank found he had to look away from her. Tears swelled in his eyes.

'No one understands you, do they? Not even your wife. She's more interested in having a baby. And whatever it is that hurt you, no matter how long ago it was, before all this trouble with the boy and his mother, it's still there, burning you, isn't it? You're holding back, but you do really want to destroy something don't you?'

'I'm not an animal...'

'I know you're not, my darling.'

'It felt good to punch that stupid boy. I enjoyed it. Once I started I couldn't stop and I just wanted to smash him into pieces. That had been building up inside me, that pure anger. It was unstoppable.'

'And you feel the same thing now?'

The breath went out of him. Heat poured over his skull, flowed like lava down his neck. Deep in his gut he felt the radiation scouring him. Acid and bleach. His fists closed. He was no more than a skeleton. White knuckles and blood seeping between his fingers. He stood up and turned to face her. She was sitting with her legs slightly apart, the material of her long faded blue dress gathered between them. With her hands planted on the wooden deck, she was leaning back, looking up at him.

He came forward and slid his knees either side of her hips, onto the hard wood, so that he was sitting astride her. She didn't resist – only kept on staring into his eyes. He was lonely no longer. In one swift movement he knocked her arms out from under her and she tumbled backwards, her head hitting the deck with a thud. She gasped but her eyes betrayed no fear. Instead they seemed to blaze with something he thought was triumph. She was right about him, she now saw.

To test her, he bent forward and brought his fingers around her throat. The flesh there was soft, like cotton. Underneath it he could feel the intricate pipework keeping her alive. Still she did not resist him.

He let go of her throat and laid his hands either side of her head, then lowered his head to her breastplate. She had on a crucifix necklace that pressed into his cheek, perhaps it would leave a permanent imprint. She brought her hands up to rest on his back.

'It's different,' he breathed. 'I want to use it. It's a strength, not a weakness.'

'Have confidence in yourself,' she said. 'The world needs to be destroyed before it can be rebuilt.'

Still, she had no name.

15

HALF-LIFE

That night the wind came scouring through the streets, bringing with it salt and death. There was nowhere to hide from it, but Frank didn't mind – he relished the way it wrapped around him, carried him along. People would have to be destroyed before the world could be rebuilt. He had been walking for some time – hours perhaps – with her words weighing on his mind. On the map of the village he held in his head, he was inscribing shapes that might, in future years, be deciphered, like hieroglyphics. Turn, turn, turn again. He was wearing his soft and quiet tennis shoes.

It was one o'clock in the morning. An hour since Alice and Anthony had driven back to her cottage on Rosehip Lane. From a shadowed doorway Frank had watched them kiss goodnight. It seemed a rather perfunctory event – did that signal some problem in their relationship? And after Anthony's departure in his put-putting little red car, Frank had slipped down the dusty path leading to a patch of allotments, from where he knew he could see Alice's bedroom window. A light, her shadow moving to and fro, then darkness.

Along the seafront, between the fisherman's huts and the piles of oyster shells, past the brewery. Alarmed, a grey cat slid through a gate. The moonlight gave it a silver stripe. Terraced houses, whitewashed cottages. Every now and then he had to throw his arm up to stifle a cough. Movement seemed to ease the pain that wracked his body. It was in his joints – the bones scratched against each other. And in his lungs fine moist nets hung, through which his breath struggled to pass. The sickness came and went as steadily as the tide.

Into the high street. Jagged black windows, dead animals on shelves, yesterday's news and the wooden floorboards of the pubs so stained with beer and blood. Imagine this place utterly deserted, abandoned. A cordon drawn around the village. No one allowed in. Radiation flowing through the streets freely, as he was doing now, dancing in through open windows, climbing into beds still warm after the hasty evacuation. There were plans for such eventualities – Frank knew them well – though in truth all those pages would tell you little more than *run, get out of there, shut it down and put up a big fence*. Thirty years hence these streets would be wild, choked with weeds, populated by wheezy gaunt foxes and the irrepressible cockroach. And how many hundreds of people would be lying in hospital beds cursing the wounded giant a couple of miles up the coast. We knew that place was evil, they'd mutter.

On Alde Street Frank stopped, turned his head slowly. He'd heard something beneath the sighs of the wind. Yes, there it was. A brisk click. A woman's heels on the pavement. But where was she? Hard to tell in which direction she was moving. He began walking towards town, avoiding the few meagre pools of light given by the street-lamps. There... Movement on the other side of the street. The woman was walking in the same direction as him, fairly fast. The sound of her heels trotting along rang out more clearly now. A tumble of hair was visible beneath her hat. At the end of the street she turned right. Frank kept low as he ran across the street and got closer to her.

They were in Harbour Road now, past the chandlers and the gates to the little boatyard. The noiseless sea was ahead of them. What business did she have being out at this time of night? Was she on some kind of night-shift, or maybe fleeing her lover?

He was less than fifty yards behind her now, but still in the darkness he could see little of her. Just a silhouette, hat and hair, coat and long dress. His breathing roared from his chest but she did not turn around. She did not know she was being followed. Of course he meant her no harm. His was a protective role; he would use his powers to keep her safe on her nocturnal trip.

She turned down a side-street, a pitiful lane with crooked cottages and a broken road surface. There were no lights here so he could just discern her figure in the centre of the road, wobbling a little in those unsuitable shoes. Then he realised that she had stopped. He did likewise. She swivelled to face him. And for a very long time they stood like that, two stick figures staring at each other, immobile, all breath and heartbeats suspended. Her malevolence clouded the street, wrapped its terrible stench around him. She would turn him to ash. All his worldly memories and plans and machinations would vanish on the wind, later to fall like nuclear rain over the village.

Then she turned away and began to walk.

Follow me, came the whisper across his mind, with that same hoarse country burr. *Follow me.*

Left at the end, towards the harbour once more. The road opened out into a broad stretch of cobbles, much stained and abused over the years. The pub was silent under its shutters, the huts were all bolted. Only the boats were alive, their masts singing as the tide sloshed against the harbour wall.

She walked over to a low rail in front of the harbour. Beyond it a ten-foot drop into the water. The moonlight spread like mercury across the stones between them. She turned to face him again. A crack went through his heart. He stopped, his legs were feeble, barely able to hold him up. The wind wrapped the green dress tight around her calves. Though she did not open her mouth, he heard her again.

He's laughing at you. He thinks you're a coward, and while you dither like a fool he will destroy that girl. She's not as strong as she sounds.

16

FISSION

Stepping out into the swirling blue day, Frank felt himself lift onto the balls of his feet, as if he were about to sprint down the path in front of him, not out of fear or haste, but simply because of the energy flowing into his legs. He had to hold himself back from running. Instead he and his escort, a burly young man with a military bearing, strode along between the sheds towards the health clinic.

He talked continually. A stream of nonsense that the other man ignored. Perhaps he was used to it. Frank could feel the radiation spreading through his body. Fizzing through him, travelling along veins and arteries and capillaries, its atoms ricocheting from bone to bone. This would give him the power he craved; he knew that. Seeing Andrea at the harbour had given him the prompt he needed. Action; life was all about action.

He looked at the other people walking around the site. Some seemed to be lost in thought, pretending to be solving some complex scientific problem while actually thinking about what was for dinner. Others looked up to issue a breezy hello and he grinned back at them. How many knew this strength? How many understood what radiation could do for them? Frank tried, surreptitiously, to peer into the eyes of a young man walking towards him, carrying a bundle of files, his sandy-coloured hair being tossed about by the wind. Are you contaminated too? he wondered. Do you feel changed too? The young man's eyes gave away nothing but of course that was the point – this was an invisible strength. No one understood it, but only Frank could identify it, use it.

There was no queue at the health clinic. A quiet day for accidents, mishaps and malingering. At Barton Hall it was well-known that if contaminated you'd get sent home for half a day, on full pay, if you so much as coughed in the presence of the nurse. Here at Seton One they seemed much more concerned with getting you back to work. Productivity was paramount.

Alice stood with her feet apart and hands on hips, and raised a quizzical eyebrow. Though there was no one else in the clinic, and a fan was blowing cool air across the room, she looked hot and harassed. Her hair was pinned mercilessly back. Pinkish maps glowed on her cheeks.

'You again. Over there,' she said, and nodded at a pristine white bed on the other side of the room. 'Shoes off. Keep everything else on.'

Frank lay back and gazed at the ceiling. It too was white, plastered, painted, cracked in several places. The room was so bright that his eyes ached. Alice made sharp metallic noises with her instruments as she prepared for the check. There was an antiseptic smell in the air that stirred in Frank some ancient memory, something subterranean yet powerful. He saw the quiet hospital ward, the screens around his mother's bed, and her face turned to the window.

Now that he was lying perfectly still, the radiation was sending little rushes of cold energy across the back of his hand, up his neck, through his scalp. It felt soothing.

'You'll get in trouble for this,' she said, approaching his bed and pulling behind her a metal trolley.

She ran a counter over him, holding the machine two inches above his body. It purred as she ran it over his hands and his face. She popped a thermometer into his mouth. A blood pressure sleeve inflated on his arm. She gave him a tissue to blow his nose and told him that he should take a shower next door. Have a good scrub.

During all of this Alice didn't once make eye contact. It was obvious that she couldn't. Because she felt him drawing strength from the radiation and she sensed that he alone knew what to do with it. How many others had passed through here, afraid and bewildered, desperately trying to expel this invisible grit from their skins? The girl was used to that. It was, he supposed, a natural reaction. Predictable and cowardly.

As she tidied up her instruments and threw a pair of rubber gloves into a rubbish bag, Frank swung his legs over the side of the bed and grinned.

'One day, you know, you'll go to a doctor's surgery and tell the doc you've got some kind of ache or pain or strife, and the doc will say, my dear fellow you simply need a buzz of this stuff. It'll do wonders for you. Make you feel twenty years younger. And he'll do exactly what you just did to me. And you'll go home and within a few hours you'll be thankful for it, and you might even have a chuckle about how worried everyone was back in the olden days, back in the dark ages. How the merest brush with radiation sent everyone scurrying to the showers. Mark my words, you'll be laughing and laughing.'

So tickled by this story was Frank that he indeed began laughing and he felt he wasn't going to stop laughing, even with Alice staring at him, not laughing, not even smiling.

He hopped off the bed and Alice took a step backwards.

'What do you want from me?' she said.

'That's the wrong question, Alice. The correct question is: what do you want me to do? How can I help you? Because I really do want to help.'

She looked like she was on the verge of tears, and he couldn't identify a good reason. Surely it was a simple enough request. Emotions, though, can be overwhelming; Gail had once told him that.

'Don't worry, I'm off to the showers for a scrub – give you some time to think it over,' said Frank.

Once behind the shower curtain he stood clear of the water. If there was any radiation on his skin he wanted to make sure it had plenty of time to be absorbed.

• • •

'Three accidents in four weeks, Frank?' said Parker.

'Luck is clearly not my lady,' Frank replied.

They were sitting in Parker's office. Frank was back in

his civvies. The earlier exhilaration of his contamination had worn off, replaced by a nausea that seemed to start in his gut and pervade all his other organs. And there was a blade digging around behind his left eyeball, trying to prise it out. Since his dismissal from the health centre he'd been told to wait in the canteen until someone came to get him. Unable to eat, Frank had sipped a cup of water and smoked cigarette after cigarette.

Parker wants to see you.

Parker wants to see you.

Parker wants to see you.

The man was a machine. A fixture. He didn't move from that desk, nor did he show any emotion, any reaction.

'We've had a report that your working methods are... unsound.'

'A report, from who?'

'I'm not at liberty to divulge that information.'

Maynard, of course. That bastard. He couldn't handle someone who sees through him, someone who interrupts his seedy little games.

'You shouldn't believe everything you hear.'

'We'll do our own checks,' said Parker.

Frank sat silently fuming.

'I don't need to tell you that your future here at Seton One is in jeopardy, Frank. I can't have workers who are a danger to themselves and others.'

An image flashed into Frank's mind, of coming home to tell Gail that he'd lost his job. There wouldn't be another chance after this; the Authority needed good scientists but there were always fresh new recruits being lined up at Cambridge. If Parker thought him a liability, he'd be out the door. And then what? Find a job with a commercial firm? Drag Gail somewhere else, after he had promised this would be their new start? Surely her patience would run out. She'd leave him, baby or no baby.

Parker was still talking, but Frank wasn't listening. He was picturing Maynard's head snapping back as his fist crashed into it. Blood and snot erupting from Maynard's nose, his stupid eyes wide with shock and terror. Begging Frank to stop. Words garbling from swollen purple lips.

Frank sat very still in his chair, luxuriating in the rush of radioactive ions around his bloodstream, feeling his power grow, gripping his knees with white knuckles. Parker was merely a bureaucratic machine; he followed protocols. There was nothing to be done about him.

Frank had to work hard to suppress his rising hysteria... Men come in all shapes and sizes and we've all been bastards in our time... Sometimes it's necessary... but men like Maynard contribute nothing... Seek only to grab what they can and to hell with the consequences. You, though, you're cleverer than he is. You see what he does to women. You can take decisive action.

And now he felt her there with him. *You did it to my worthless son didn't you? Jumbled his face up – not that he didn't deserve it, and that gives you the advantage. You've stepped over the line. Me too. Anything is possible now, Frank.*

17

RELEASE

Judy swirled ice cubes around her glass, screwed up her eyes. Uh-oh, thought Gail, here comes something serious.

'Is Frank all right?' Judy said. Her worried tone hit a false note that was starting to become familiar. She was just being nosey. 'I only say it – and absolutely do stop me if this is just far too uncomfortable for you – because I saw him yesterday and he just looked so, well what's the word, *troubled*. He just looked straight through me. Like I wasn't there.'

'He's fine,' Gail said quickly. She wasn't keen to open up this particular topic. 'Probably just preoccupied with work.'

They were sitting on Judy's patio enjoying the softening late afternoon sunshine. Lucy was playing on the dusty lawn with a collection of driftwood, making camps for her dolls. William was in his bedroom. The men would be home soon. At least that was the theory. Both Maynard and Frank seemed to be working extra hours recently. Something about commissioning new equipment. Gail had her doubts about the veracity of this excuse, she'd never known Frank consistently work late at any other time.

Judy tried another angle.

'He's a good man, your Frank. And he's got a mischievous side to him – an edge. I like that.'

Yes, I've noticed you liking that, thought Gail, though her jealousy was shot with humour rather than anger.

'Not like my oaf of a husband,' Judy went on. 'God, what a catch I thought I had. And look at him now – trapped, miserable, pawing any young girl unfortunate enough to come into his radius. He'll make a fool of himself with this Alice. You watch; it's all so predictable. I mean, what is it with men and younger women?'

'Search me. Recapturing past glories maybe? Exerting their power? Do you think I've got all this to come with Frank?'

'No, no. There's something different about Frank. The way he looks at you. I caught him once or twice the other night; it's such an adoring look. So sweet. He wasn't looking at Alice the way he was looking at you.'

Gail spread her hands in the air and sighed, as if to say, who could ever understand the motives of others? 'He's a man, with all the problems associated.'

'But what does he want? Out of life, I mean.'

'His family are totally messed up. His mother was in and out of psychiatric institutions throughout his childhood and then killed herself when he was eighteen. His father was a tyrant, as far as I can tell, a bully. It was probably him that drove her to suicide, though he blamed Frank. Said that Frank's behaviour placed an intolerable burden of worry on his mother. As soon as he could Frank left for university and never went back, not even for Christmas holidays. Barely spoke to his father for ten years.'

'Jesus, I don't blame him. His father sounds awful.'

'But it was so unhealthy for Frank. It would have been better to have a blazing row. Instead, he's bottled it all up, all that grief. And it's still eating him up. I worry about him.'

'You think he's going to make himself ill like his mother?'

'I don't know. No, probably not that. What I find worrying is that he has these black and white versions of his parents in his head – his mother the saint, his father the demon. And sometimes he'll say something that makes me think he sees everyone in these terms. That all women are kind and gentle and have hobbies like watercolour painting – which is what his mother did apparently – and all men are violent brutes.'

Judy was silent. God, does she agree with that view? Gail wondered. Does she see Maynard as just that violent bully?

And Gail remembered Frank's eyes that night, when he came home covered in the boy's blood, and it wasn't the calmness of his expression that so terrified her but the glittering triumph.

'Would you ever bring up a baby alone?' Judy said.

'Christ no...no, No...'

'And yet some women don't have the choice.'

Not being entirely honest there, are you? Gail thought. It's not as if you haven't considered it, even made some plans for it. Where you'd go, what you'd do for money. There's even the bank account in Oxford you set up before you left. She pictured the man in the Lamb and Flag, looking over from the bar. Yes, she thought, your life need not end here.

• • •

They were in the living room, listening to the evening concert, when Andrea's instruction came to him.

Get up, if you want to do anything good in your life, get up and follow.

Startled, Frank looked over at Gail. But she was curled up on an armchair with her nose in a book and betrayed no sign of having heard a voice.

Andrea seemed to be speaking to him from the radio, her voice woven into the music itself. At first he couldn't react, bewildered and rigid in his armchair, staring at the radio.

Get moving, she hissed. *If you're capable, get moving.* And now her voice was close behind his right ear, intimate yet sharp. Instinctively he turned to look for her, but knew straightaway she wouldn't be there. The voice was real, that was beyond dispute, but there was nothing physical of it in the room. She had found a way to connect with him in some other mysterious way, and he accepted that.

He stood and moved to the window, peered through the crack in the curtains.

The girl's in danger.

And sure enough, Maynard's front door was opening

and the beast came lumbering out. Frank felt revulsion at the idea of Maynard touching Alice. Spoiling her. She was really just a child, unaware of what she was getting herself into.

You can't let it happen, you must stop him, stop him, stop him.

Her voice was becoming more piercing. It cut into him like the blade she'd marked him with. He clutched his fingers to his temple, willing her to be quiet but unable to quell her anger. In the sliver of window he could see his grimacing reflection.

Beyond, Maynard was getting into his car.

Move. You owe me this. After everything you've done to my family.

'You all right over there?' said Gail.

'Fine,' he said, trying to keep his voice neutral while his thoughts accelerated.

'Come and sit down. Tell me more about your day.'

'I just need to go out for a bit,' he said, still with his back to her. He daren't turn around for fear she'd see something terrible in his face.

'Out? Where out? You sure you're all right?'

'Gail, I just need to do something, I can't...'

And he was already tripping out of the room, unable to look his wife in the eye, drawn by Andrea's siren call to leave the house, get in his car and follow Maynard.

18

CHAIN REACTION

Sitting in his car, two hundred yards down from Alice's cottage, nausea bloomed into Frank's throat.

Maynard could not get away with this kind of behaviour. Granted, it was not unusual among men of his type. The louts who dominated their wives, fucked around on the side, bullied their colleagues. The type who threw balls around at the weekend rather than playing with their children. Who took a belt to their son. That belt of his father's, with its dull brass buckle, so smooth to the touch but so easily slicing the skin on his thighs.

That such behaviour was commonplace made it even more offensive. There was a casual entitlement to it, an assumption that it would go unchallenged. After all, hadn't Maynard told him to keep his mouth shut about his affair with Alice? And hadn't he obeyed?

As his mother used to say to him, actions speak louder than words.

Alice came hurrying down the passageway beside her house. Had she climbed out of her bedroom window to make a secret escape? Silly girl. She got into Maynard's car and it pulled away.

Driving without headlights was a difficult business. Being closer to Maynard would have made it easier to follow the contours of the road, but Frank didn't want to risk being seen. So he held back in the darkness, crouching over the steering wheel, his fingers twitchy, his palms greasy. It wasn't completely pitch; the last embers of a summer's day are slow to fade, and the moon was fat. Still, the tension coiled through him.

Andrea's voice had now deserted him. He missed its surety of purpose. Without it, doubts prodded him. But no, he would not be deterred. If he was alone, so be it. It helped to imagine his mother and father in that car ahead. How much molecular difference was there between two human beings after all? His father could be Maynard. Maynard could be his father. They seemed to think alike. They certainly acted alike.

I am not my father.

My father is in that car ahead.

My mother too, the unknowing. The victim-to-be of his casual, pointless cruelty.

Yes! Now you understand.

Andrea's return was so loud and shattering that in shock he wrenched the steering wheel to one side, swerved across the lane with a sickening squeal, and only just prevented the car from launching itself into a neighbouring meadow.

We are the same, you and I. We cannot go back.

The rear lights of the big Rover flashed in and out of view as it took the slow twisting turns of the coast road, heading south. Frank did not want to go back. If he was driving into some kind of oblivion, so be it. Courage demanded that he follow this course.

• • •

Alice stretched out her legs, ruffling her skirt up over her knees. He looked over and raised his eyebrows.

'What are you doing to me?'

'Just keep your eyes on the road sunshine,' she replied. 'Where are we going anyway?'

'Up Rendlegay Bank. There's somewhere we can park up there. Nice and quiet.'

She hadn't slept with him yet, but it seemed tonight was the night. Why the fuck not? And afterwards she could tell him how he compared to his mate Anthony. Now that she knew Maynard better, a little better anyway, she felt some of the comments she'd heard about him were unfair. He wanted life, wanted energy and sex and dancing. Not nappies, and boring dinner parties, and a wife who would only do it once a month in bed in the dark. He hadn't forgotten what it felt like to be young. He was clinging on to that memory and trying to reanimate it. He wanted a girl who made him feel alive. Yes, it was a cliché – the mid-life crisis – but weren't most clichés based in truth?

The affair was tentative, new, and of course secretive. Trying to see each other was an elaborate game, because not only did he have a wife to hide the affair from, but none of their colleagues could know either. A fun game, though she could see it would eventually become exasperating. Perhaps that was when these sorts of affairs stopped – when the disappointments outweighed the pleasures.

Now, though, it was exciting. Their bodies were magnetised. Pulled together. She loved the sense of his age and experience, his physical strength and capability. And even though she wanted nothing to do with kids until she was at least thirty, the idea that he'd already fathered children added another chemical into the compound. He was a man, not a boy.

The road dipped and curved behind the line of sand dunes. She knew it well enough. Her uncle used to have a place in the next village. The big car's headlights picked out sand streaked across the tarmac, whitened long grass, a startled fox. It was a warm night but out here the wind would be cutting. If she was going to get undressed she'd be doing it inside the car, with the heater on.

She recognised a derelict farmhouse, a sharp bend in the road. She'd been here before, with another boy. A boy, not a man. For some reason she thought of Gail hanging around outside the doctor's, that look of desolation on her face, as if she was staring at a future that could never be hers. But Alice felt that it would happen for Gail. That strange husband of hers would come up with the goods. He was a good one, once you scratched the surface. And what would it be like to have another life growing in your belly? What if Maynard got her pregnant tonight?

He swung the car off the road and she felt the tyres struggling for grip in the sand. Then they were stopped, engine and lights off, her cigarette smoke filling the silence between them. Through the windscreen she could just make out the horizon between two sand dunes. The sea had the same hum as the power station. Maynard opened his door, walked around the car and opened hers.

With a little help, she wiggled her bottom up onto the warm bonnet of the car. Maynard stood at the bumper facing her. The engine still seemed alive beneath her. His fingers encircled her ankles, then began sliding up her bare shins. As they began to kiss she heard the faint sound of another car in the distance.

His tongue was rough and insistent, his hands probing. She squirmed, not precisely out of fear – more because she felt caught off-guard – his lust was only just under control and the wind was picking up, blowing her hair across both their faces while the sea groaned, revved... No, that was the car again, much closer. It was coming towards them, but there were no lights. Why were there no lights? She tried to shove Maynard away but he pushed back. Creak of tyres on sand. Someone had come after them. An explosion of light. Maynard, old and fat in this harsh glare, staggered backwards from her and stood blinking into the light, apparently unable to process what was going on. Alice slid off the bonnet and yanked her clothing back into place.

'What the...' Maynard started saying.

Alice stepped out of the pool of light and tried to make out the shape behind the wheel. For an awful moment nothing happened. The three of them (she presumed their pursuer was alone) did not move or speak. The car had stopped only a few inches behind Maynard's, blocking him in. Its engine was still running.

The driver's door opened and a figure rose and stood beside the car. It was a man's shape but seemed to be cloaked in black. She could see nothing of his face.

He issued a single word: 'Run.'

She backed away, unsure what to do. Maynard was still rooted to the spot, dumbfounded. Terror twisted through her, erased words from her mind. She turned and ran blindly across the sand dune, tripped and veered to the gap where she'd seen the horizon. There was open space to run into. The beach, the beach would save her.

• • •

'What the hell are you doing?' shouted Maynard. He staggered from the darkness into the light of the headlights, holding his forearm over his eyes and squinting, yet it was still possible to see the disgusting lust in his face. His cheeks were red and a vein bulged at his temple. His shirt was unbuttoned at his chest. Frank remained calm.

'Leave her alone,' he said.

'Turn those fucking lights off you maniac.'

Frank repeated his command.

'Did you follow us here? Are you some kind of peeping tom?'

'Leave her…'

'Stop saying that. Fuck, I told you to keep your mouth shut and not interfere didn't I? What's the matter? Have you fallen in love? Is that it? Jealous, are you?'

He's a cunt, teach him a lesson. Now!

Frank sprang forward and swung his fist upwards, crashing into Maynard's throat. Maynard swayed backwards and made a glurgle sound, and then Frank swung again and again, wildly, freely, joyously, the energy pouring out through his arms, sometimes connecting with the other man's face, sometimes his skull, sometimes missing entirely. Maynard stayed on his feet longer than that boy had, but when he fell he fell hard. He didn't even put his hands out to brace the fall, just landed with a thwump on his face. Frank stood, gazing down at the inert body, gathering in his breathing, flexing his blood-stained fingers.

Then he looked up at the heavens and was enclosed in their silent roar. The universe approved. And after all, they were only specks of dust. Who would miss them? Whispering over the black surface of the ocean came her voice again. Impatient, almost exasperated, as if she was disappointed in him. *Finish it, put him away, put him under. I don't want to look at him for another moment.*

Obeying her was the only certainty Frank had left. Theirs was a special relationship forged in the heat of blood. He so wanted to please her.

In the boot of his car he unfastened the tool kit and slid out the metal jack. It was cool and reassuringly solid in his palm.

You have no choice now. Your path is set.

When he came back to the front of the car he found that Maynard had come to and was sitting cross-legged in the sand. From out of the bloody mess of his face, his eyes stared up at Frank, dull and uncomprehending. He looked ridiculous, pathetic. Sitting there like a child in nursery, trying to be good for teacher. Too fucking late.

Frank swung the jack into the side of his head and after Maynard crumpled sideways back to the earth, Frank went on slamming the jack against the side of his skull until he felt it soften and finally collapse.

• • •

The land, previously flat, seemed to be folding in on itself. Only by swaying backwards and forwards could Frank stay on his feet. He felt suddenly cold. Lacerated by a fierce wind that extinguished the stars in the sky and whipped sand into his mouth and eyes. Alone. He'd never felt so alone. The body at his feet was just a lump of gristle and bone. Andrea had gone; he knew it. Her presence had been sucked away, entwined with Maynard's spirit. Instead of her there were hundreds of predatory birds, clawing the branches of nearby trees, snarling in hungry delight. They wanted the body. And afterwards they'd attack him.

But he wouldn't let them have their feast.

He climbed the grassy dune in front of Maynard's car and looked down at the beach. It was, as far as he could tell, empty. Alice would be running back to the village if she had any sense. It was a long way – five miles, probably – but still he had to work quickly. She might go straight to the police, or more likely, to the pub where her brother drank. Frank knew what he was going to do.

The sea was inky and still, its power withheld. It would claim Maynard, snatch him from the glistening sand, toss him about in its currents.

For a moment, he imagined it was his father's body lying there. That sad old bastard wouldn't have gone so easily; he was indestructible. He still lived in the same house, slept in the same bed, shuffled around the same garden. Was he haunted too? Did the bedclothes fasten themselves a noose around his neck at night? No, Frank's mother was too kind a soul to haunt anyone; she was gone too – whispered away.

Just getting the body up into roughly a sitting position was hard enough. It was as though it was magnetised to the ground. Frank figured a fireman's lift was the best way to move it around. He managed to get his hands under Maynard's armpits to hold him steady, but as he prepared to lift, the smashed head lolled forward. A couple of flies were already showing some interest – a distraction he could have done without. Planting his feet wide apart, Frank began to heave upwards.

Once Maynard was up on his feet, despite the searing pain in his shoulders and arms, Frank knew he had to keep lifting. The radiation gave him strength to keep going. He got the other man up onto his shoulder, but as soon as he had fastened his arms around Maynard's thighs the change to the weight distribution unshipped him. He stumbled backwards, lost his footing, and fell. The body plunged head-first to the ground and Frank ended up in a tangle of legs, cursing vehemently.

He tried again, making sure to keep his feet as far apart as possible. Yes. Up and up and steady; steady. Once he'd got the body onto his shoulder he paused, stabilised, then began to trudge slowly towards the sea.

Between the dunes, down into the soft corrugations, towards the waves. Soon his feet sank into wet sand. Maynard felt heavier than ever. But the cleansing sea wind urged him on, whistling about his ears and singing to his wildness. The elements were on his side. They wanted to swallow up this nasty business. The heavens approved of Frank's heroism, understood the necessity of what he'd done. Now let the sea make it vanish.

When water came up to his knees, electrifyingly cold, Frank stopped. Heaved Maynard off his shoulder and laid him down. He stood there, gazing at the lifeless lump being washed by the indifferent waves. His features were blurred by death. There was no sound from his throat, no malice behind the eyelids Frank had himself stroked shut. To die so quickly was a mercy.

He walked slowly back to the cars, suddenly feeling ever so tired.

On the front seat of Maynard's car lay Alice's handbag, which he picked up and placed in the boot of his own car. Then, working methodically, he checked every other space inside Maynard's car, looking for any other signs that she'd been there. Nothing. Good.

Using a torch Frank then circled Maynard's car, examining the ground. A cigarette butt with lipstick marks went into his pocket. Some indentations in the sand that could have been her footprints (he hadn't seen what shoes she was wearing) he scrubbed out using a twig. Finally he came around to the place where Maynard had fallen. In the harsh glare of the torch the blood looked purple and viscous. It had sprayed over a wide space. It was possible that the wind would blow sand over it, but he couldn't depend on that, so he spent several minutes gathering up scoops of it in his hands and depositing them into a thick bush close to the road. Then he retraced his steps, using the twig to obscure his footprints, doing a reverse lap of Maynard's car in this fashion, until he was able to climb back into his own car.

Sitting there behind the wheel, he was overcome with exhaustion. All the anger and purpose and malice had flowed out of him. In its place was a thin sadness. The pointlessness of it all was so crushing. Damage upon damage. Death and oblivion were inevitable.

PART THREE

19

ENERGY

Hot pain in her chest, knees buckling under her, the sea and wind and sand spinning across her, Alice fell, scrambled to her knees, crawled, then stopped. She was safe. She didn't need to flee. At least, not right now. But safe from what, from who? Who was it who had followed them? It wasn't Georgie, her brother. She'd have recognised the voice and his stature. And he would have told her to get in his car, not to run. Besides, it just wasn't his style.

Anthony? Could he really be that jealous? It seemed incredible. But not impossible. Once, just once, she'd seen him angry and the force of it had surprised her.

She peered into the darkness, up towards the dunes and the cars. The headlights of the second car were still on, a muffled and grainy glow. She strained to listen for shouting but the sea obliterated all. The sea always had the last word. Then the headlights went out. There was nothing but blue-black emptiness.

What did that mean?

Trying to pace herself, she ran through the heavy sand. When the coastline curved a little she could see the cluster of lights that was her home village. They looked a long, long way off. Just as her exhaustion grew, her fear diminished. Whoever it was back there wasn't coming after her. Hadn't he told her to run?

Though it was a warm night the wind on the beach was sharp and she wore only a cotton dress and flimsy cardigan. Her shoes were full of sand. On she trudged, following the intersection of sea, land and sky, each a different hue of black. Oh bloody hell, what was going on back there? Who was it? Someone who wanted to scare Maynard away from her. Who had the right to do that? No man, that was for sure. And yet that was what men did – squabbled over girls, tried to piss on each other's fires. Even older, intelligent men who should know better. It was pathetic.

So not Anthony, not her brother, then who? One of the lads from the village? It was possible, but most of them had given up on her as a lost cause, and besides, how would they know about her and Maynard? It had to be someone at the power station. As she realised, her stomach knotted. Frank. Yes, of course. The way he'd looked at her that day in the alleyway behind the generators, his weird lunge at Maynard at the dinner party. And he was dangerous. Maynard had told her the rumour going round the power station that Frank had been fired from his last job after a fight in which he'd almost killed another man. And wasn't there something about his eyes? Something detached and terrifying, like he was judging everybody, and if you came up short he had no sympathy for you at all. Nothing. No moderation, no balance. Like you were either with him or against him. Alice remembered catching him staring at Maynard during the dinner party and how, at the time, she'd wondered what was going through his head. Better not to know. What did Gail see in him? She was so lovely and he was so...stiff and repressed. Even for a scientist he was cold.

She stopped and looked back, but there was only darkness. The waves went on thrumming at the shore. If it was Frank, what did that mean for Maynard? Would they fight? Surely Maynard would get the better of him? She tried to picture them throwing punches at each other, then wrestling in the sand, grunting like animals, and she derived no sense of pride from the images. Some girls liked men to fight over them but that was just vanity. Stupidity too, for the fight implied that the girl was an object to be possessed or a territory to be conquered.

Let the silly sods fight. She would have no more to do with them.

Now her feet crunched across an expanse of shells, mostly razor-clams. The beach here was slim and shone wet in the moonlight. The tide was coming in. Ahead the village sparkled like a Christmas tree toppled with all its lights on, and beyond it was the eerie glow of Seton One.

After walking four miles along the beach it felt strange to tread on the hard surface of a road again. Her feet were sore and soggy, sand scraped at her instep, her calves burnt and her head was pounding. She guessed it wasn't far off last orders in the pubs, and headed along the harbour road to The Anchor. It looked inviting, with its honeyed light cast out into the street and the glint of bottles upon the windows. Yet the deep male hum of conversation, and the occasional drunken shout, stopped her from going in. Any girl going into that place had to be ready to defend herself from leery comments and grabbing hands, and she just couldn't face it. Georgie would be slumped in the back corner of the lounge bar with his mates and she'd have to run the gauntlet to get his attention. And then what? Explain that she'd been having an affair with a married man with kids... That another married man had been following them and had interrupted them just before... That they may have had a fight but she didn't know for sure. Oh, fuck no. Even if she could persuade Georgie to get off his lazy fat arse and drive up there, the most likely scenario was that he would punch Maynard too.

Alice turned and walked around the harbour to the phone box. Shut the door and slumped against one side. It smelt of piss and stale cigarette smoke but at least it hadn't been vandalised. She picked up the receiver and dialled 999.

'Police,' she croaked when asked which service she required. It took a moment to connect.

'Police. What's the emergency?'

'There's been a fight,' she said, and immediately regretted doing so. How did she know what had happened?

'Where was this fight?'

'On the coast road, south of Setonisle.'

'On the road?' The woman sounded sceptical. 'And this fight has finished? Is anyone hurt?'

'Well, I... I don't know.'

'Where are you please?'

'I'm in the village. In Setonisle I mean.'

'And you witnessed this fight?'

'Well, no... I... Oh look, forget it. It doesn't matter.'

'Miss...'

Alice replaced the receiver and pushed her way out of the phone box. She just wanted to climb into her bed and pull the covers over her head.

20

HEAT

The first things he saw, waking from a short dreamless sleep, were Gail's eyes. The blue of her irises seemed to be softening as she got older, and fine creases appearing underneath her eyes. She wore spectacles for reading now, and rarely looked more attractive than curled up, feline, with a book in her lap and her spectacles slipped down her nose.

'Good morning sleepyhead,' she said, with a smile. 'It's almost eight o'clock. You'll be late for work.'

He made a grunting sound that he hoped conveyed that he acknowledged this information and didn't care about work. It had been so hot that they'd taken to sleeping with a sheet instead of a duvet, and in the mornings it was either stuffed down the end of the bed or, as now, tangled around their ankles.

'You were late last night,' she said. 'I miss you when you're not here.'

Images began to play across his mind. Maynard's dead mass on the wet sand. Alice's figure dashing away. Where would the body be now? Under the waves, or washed up on a beach somewhere. What if he'd got it wrong about the tide? What if Maynard hadn't been dragged out to sea but was still lying there, his wounds washed clean, his limbs draped in seaweed?

'I'm not going to lose you am I?' Gail said.

'What? Of course not. I would never leave you,' Frank said, astonished at the very question. 'Why do say that?'

'I didn't say leave, I said lose. Into here, I mean.' And she tapped his head.

Not knowing how to respond, he looked at her for some time, gazing at the face he'd come to know and love. He could barely remember the time before Gail. He was a selfish fucker, she'd told him often enough – sometimes affectionately, sometimes not. Yet she was delicate too, in her own way, and she needed him.

'I hope not,' he said finally – three words that silenced her for a moment.

'We can make it work here can't we?' she said.

'I think so.'

'And start a family? I want to have babies, your babies.'

'Let's just...'

'What?'

'Settle down first. Here, I mean.'

He swung his legs off the bed and sat for a moment, assessing the protests various parts of his body were sending to his brain. The muscles in his calves and shoulders ached. His gut was tight. His throat was sore.

Last night he'd sat in his car for some time, mind obliterated, wind screaming round and round. And then he'd realised that Alice might call the police, or drag her brother out of the pub, and bring them to Maynard's car. And if they were quicker than the tide, they might find Maynard's body. The idea of moving Maynard appalled him, so Frank decided to move Maynard's car to – hopefully – confuse Alice. The keys were still in the ignition of the big Rover, so Frank drove it two miles further up the coast, away from the village and parked it in a neat hiding spot behind a wall of bulrushes. Then, after giving it another check for incriminating evidence, he walked briskly back to his car, all the time fearing that a car's headlights would come sweeping through the darkness to pick him out, but none such came.

As he sat on the bed rubbing his forehead with his palms, he wondered what Judy was doing, across the road. What her reaction would be to waking to an empty bed. Frank felt giddy. He screwed his eyes shut, just like when he was six years old, and when he opened them again nothing had changed. He went to run a bath.

As he lay with water up to his chin, Gail came in and sat on the toilet, sighing her relief as she pissed.

'Are you going in with Maynard this morning?' she said.

Frank shook his head. He'd run the water as hot as he could take it in the hope it might ease his aching body. The idea of going to work was atrocious to him, yet he knew he had to make the effort.

'You know, Judy says he likes you...you know, despite all that crap the other night.'

'I'm not sure I believe that,' he said.

'He's probably just intimidated by you,' she said. 'Promise me you'll just try one more time. We do have to live opposite them. It will make things quite awkward if you two don't get on.'

'I'll knock for him.'

Having neither the stomach nor the time for breakfast, as he got dressed Frank slurped down the cup of milky tea Gail had made him, tossed half a packet of biscuits into his briefcase and left the house. Strode across the tarmac. Better not to over-think it, just block out what's happened and return to normal. Waiting for Judy to answer the door, he realised he was shivering. Indeed there was a surprising chill in the air. Was summer turning prematurely to autumn? Had the weather gods been watching him last night?

She was dressed but dishevelled, bleary-eyed, not from crying – he guessed – but lack of sleep. Frank felt a confusing swirl of revulsion and sympathy for her. For a moment she simply stared and panic rose in him. What did she know? But then he remembered what Maynard had once said about the way lack of sleep, night after night, messes with your brain.

'I just…'

'He's not here,' Judy cut in. 'His car's not here. He didn't come home last night.'

'Oh, umm…'

'I don't suppose you've got any idea where he is?' she said, and her tone was blunt, with more than a hint of accusation. Rather than worried, she was angry. She knew about his dalliances with other women; she wasn't daft. And she considered all men part of the same sleazy club.

Frank shook his head, and something in the look on his face seemed to give her some reassurance that he was telling the truth, because her expression relaxed a little.

'No, no, there's no reason why you would. Sorry. It's just that I've been up all night. It's not like him to not come home. And with the car too.'

'He couldn't have gone to stay with a friend? Something he forgot to tell you about?'

'No. It's more likely that he's in bed with some tart and too drunk to move. Too drunk or too happy. In the unlikely event that he turns up to work, will you please tell him to phone his wife?'

And before Frank could say another word, Judy shut the door.

• • •

Waking in a fug, with cracked lips and crusted eyes, Alice heard the sea and scrambled, afraid, out of bed, then stood swaying and squinting in her bedroom, slowly coming to her senses. She was in her room, not on the beach. Daylight glowed underneath her curtains. There was no one after her. She sat down and gulped down water from the glass beside her bed. It hadn't been there when she fell asleep – her father must have brought it up for her when he came to bed. He always checked on her before he turned in, even now. A daddy's girl.

She tried to replay last night's events but sleep had not helped to clarify the images. What she did remember, however, was the conclusion she'd come to during that long walk home; that it was Frank who'd followed them there, who'd shouted to her to run. And what of Maynard?

She'd been a coward. She should have stayed with him and faced whatever came. To hell with the consequences.

Jesus, Alice, she thought, you think of yourself as a rebel, as different, and yet when there's a whiff of scandal you run a mile. Literally run a mile.

She was ashamed of herself, and wanted to see Maynard to say sorry.

Skipping breakfast, Alice had a quick bath, dressed and ran a brush through her hair, then cycled to the power station where she stopped, breathless, in the car park. His car was not in its usual spot. She stared at the empty space for some time, circled the rest of the car park but the Rover wasn't there. It was quarter past nine. Perhaps he was running late? She knew this wasn't true.

During her morning break she sneaked back to the car park, but another car had taken Maynard's space. At lunchtime he wasn't to be seen in the canteen. Anthony was there, eating alone, though she could hardly ask him about Maynard's whereabouts.

Gradually a hole opened beneath her – a bottomless space without reason, without constraints – a darkness that could only be death. She felt it in the pit of her stomach.

• • •

It wasn't too hard for Frank to keep himself busy. The good thing about his line of work was that it could be very absorbing. It was easy to lose yourself in the minutiae of reactor pile behaviour. It was a world in itself, and while he wasn't king of that world, he did feel a kind of watchful power over it. Only a few people in the world could understand what was going on underneath that microscope of his.

There were no immediate signs of Maynard being missed at work. At lunchtime Frank sat with Anthony, and felt he had better mention his morning conversation with Judy – it would have been odd if he hadn't. Anthony just shrugged. He had other things on his mind. A couple of days earlier Alice had told him their relationship was over. In all the intensity of the last day or so, Frank had completely forgotten about Anthony's plight. He wanted to say, things disintegrate, people fall apart, but he knew this wouldn't be consolation for the poor bloke. After forcing down a child-size portion of shepherd's pie, Frank wandered off to have a cigarette down beside the reactor building, by the fence that gave a view of the sea.

The earlier chill had burnt off. Yet again it was a blazing hot day, with a creamy gauze at the horizon. The sea was as placid as it had been last night. You did the right thing, he told himself. You saved her. That's all that matters. Not everyone will understand, but that's your lot now. You are a protector of the weak. It will be, in effect, a secret life. His mask was quietness. Look out for the quiet ones, didn't they say? But no one ever really did.

• • •

The police car outside Judy and Maynard's house was a little modern thing, pale blue and white with shiny chrome bumpers. Seeing it there, the bright reality of it, made Frank feel uneasy. It was all very well him sitting at work thinking about how relaxed he was, how clear his story was, and how everything he'd done had a valid reason. But he was assuming the police would respond in an entirely logical way. Assumptions, he had learnt long ago, were dangerous things.

'Maynard is missing,' Gail said, as soon as he came into the kitchen where she was cooking, a large glass of gin within easy reach.

'Still?'

'What do you mean still? How do you know about it?'

Frank took a moment to let the two versions of events – real and constructed – swim apart, so he could confidently say the right thing. He was tired, he'd been suffering stomach cramps all day, and the aches in his body seemed to be intensifying rather than easing. Maintaining his story under questioning wouldn't be a problem, he realised, but it was in moments like these that he could be caught off-guard.

'I went to knock for him this morning, didn't I?' he said, after a lengthy pause. Fortunately Gail was too pissed to notice his hesitation.

'Oh God, yes. What was Judy like then? He's been gone since last night; never came home.'

'Well, she was worried, I suppose?' Frank said, throwing in some theatrical uncertainty.

'She barely slept all night,' Gail said. 'When she came round here she was frantic – really panicking. But what could I do? I made her go and have a lie-down this afternoon before the school run. I think she got a bit of sleep, but she wouldn't touch a drop of booze. Quite a relief to get back here and hit the gin, truth be told. She thinks something bad has happened to him.'

Frank hesitated, watching Gail. She was keeping something from him, and she was afraid.

'What makes her think that?'

Gail looked down, avoiding his eyes. 'Oh, just that it's so out of character.'

'People are capable of much stranger things than other people think they are,' replied Frank. While Gail went on stirring her pot, he went upstairs to get changed. He spent ten minutes making the bed, putting washed clothes away and giving the bathroom a quick clean.

• • •

The policeman looked pale and rather harassed. His voice, as he asked Frank if he minded answering a few questions, implied that he couldn't really be bothered, but knew he had to do his duty. Perhaps he'd already made up his mind about Maynard. Perhaps he knew Judy would be watching from her window.

Frank showed him through to the living room, where Gail was sitting demurely in an armchair. She'd tidied herself up for their visitor, brushed her hair, put on some lipstick. The policeman nodded respectfully and took the seat Frank indicated. He was young, in his twenties, wearing a white shirt and dark-blue tie. Around his close-shaved head ran a faint red line where his helmet had been sitting. Frank watched him to see if he paid Gail any undue attention, but didn't pick up any such signals. The poor lad was probably still recovering from being with Judy. He didn't take a cup of tea but accepted a glass of water.

'You work with Mr Scott at the plant?'

'I do. Well, we're not in the same area. We both work there – that's about it. We have lunch together quite often.'

'And what do you do there?' asked the policeman.

'Sorry, I can't tell you that,' Frank said, trying not to sound sanctimonious.

'Sir, a man has gone missing.'

'I understand that,' said Frank. 'But nevertheless I can only tell you about my work if we are on Ministry property, and with the appropriate representation.'

Surely he knew that? Was he just trying to see how reliable Frank was?

'I don't really see what the big secret is,' the policeman grumbled.

'Then the system is working pretty well, isn't it?' said Frank, affecting a smile that he hoped was conciliatory. As the policeman looked down at his notes, Gail stared at him. Her knuckles glared white, so tightly were her hands clamped together.

The questions were perfunctory. Easy to answer, and for the most part truthfully. Gail kept quiet other than to confirm that she was friends with Judy and sometimes helped with the children. And yes, wasn't it all so worrying. He seemed like such a normal chap, not prone to running off or anything. Her use of the past tense when referring to Maynard sent a tremor through Frank but the policeman didn't react. Did she suspect he was dead?

'What will happen now?' Gail asked once the questions were over. 'I suppose it's just a case of waiting?'

'I expect so,' said the policeman, as if he wasn't quite sure himself. 'We'll see what happens.'

'I'll show you out,' said Frank.

Gail disappeared into the kitchen and the two men made their way down the hallway to the front door. Before Frank could open the door, the policeman held up his hand and bent forward.

'If you don't mind me asking, and just between you and me, what kind of man is he – Mr Scott?' he said, taking care to keep his voice low.

'What kind of man? Well, he's a family man, a hard worker. Loves his car. Pretty normal, really.'

'Sir, you can talk plainly. This won't go any further. My understanding is that he's something of an egoist, well-known in the pubs in the village for chasing girls and bragging about his work. You kept your confidentiality just now. He most certainly does not.'

'You think he's done a bunk?'

'I really couldn't say, sir.'

Frank stood on his front step, watching the policeman lope back to his little car, aware that Judy and other neighbours were probably watching. Then, squinting into the setting sun, he thought about his wife's suspicions and what he should do about her. He stepped back into the house and closed the door.

• • •

Gail made a dinner of sausages and fried potatoes, but neither of them was hungry and the plates of food sat unfinished on the table. In silence, smoking, she watched him for signs of…well, she wasn't sure what, and she feared what she might see. Frank did not look at her. He was sitting hunched forward, staring at the fat congealing on his plate, taking short sucks on his cigarette with a shaking hand. His skin looked grey and his scar glistened.

During Andrea's trial, which had gone on forever because of problems with the jury, and had been covered in every newspaper, Gail had tried to shut herself away from the world, to focus on Frank's recovery, protecting him from the pain of seeing that woman again. While the rest of the world hungered for details of Andrea's dysfunctional family and her vengeful violence, Gail didn't want to know any details about her husband's attacker. For Gail, Andrea was just a manifestation of Frank's original crime – part of the backlash, a scar just like the one she'd carved in his face. Andrea was crude and awful and not to become part of their lives.

He frowned.

'That woman who attacked you, she did this to you, didn't she? She's changed you.'

'What are you talking about?' he said. But he knew.

She began to cry. 'Where's *my* Frank? The man I knew and loved. Where has he gone?'

'Nothing's changed,' he said quietly.

'Everything's changed!' Gail screamed. 'Every fucking thing has changed. You beat a boy nearly to death, then you get yourself cut up, and we come out here to make a fresh start, to have a family for fuck's sake... And now... what? What exactly has happened now? You tell me.'

'Stop shouting, you're hurting my head.'

'No Frank, I will not stop shouting. You went out last night on your own. You came back late. Maynard is missing. The police are involved. So you tell me, what is going on?'

'What is this? An interrogation? Are you joining the police, Gail?'

'Frank, I'm scared. Please talk to me.'

'It's not her. Don't blame her, it's not her fault. She only wants what's right.'

'Who?' Gail said, and then realising who he meant, struggled to say her name. 'Andrea? Is that who you mean?'

How on earth did Frank think he knew what Andrea wanted? The woman was in prison.

Frank stood up and gripped the edge of the table, his eyes aflame.

'She understands me better than you, better than anyone. When I hear her voice I feel like...like finally there's someone who understands me and is on my side. She doesn't laugh at me or pay lip service to my ideas. She sees my strength.'

Fear and confusion clamped down on Gail. She opened her lips to respond, but no words came. The only thought in her mind was *what do you mean?* And after he'd said that she didn't understand him, how could she say that? The four words sat on her tongue like a polished pebble, then dissolved to sand.

'You've never seen it, have you Gail?' His anger had dissipated. 'You've never seen what I'm capable of.'

'How does she talk to you? She's in prison. Does she write to you? No, I would have seen the letters, so does she write to you at the power station? Is that how you keep your secrets?'

Frank laughed and shook his head. He took his plate over to the sink and left the room. Gail put her face in her hands and began to sob.

21

PRESSURE

He saw her briefly the next morning, crossing the road between the health clinic and the administration building. He couldn't be sure it was her; there were several young girls around the place and with their hair hidden and wearing white uniforms they all looked the same from a distance. Let her go, he told himself, and instead of going into the canteen as he'd been about to, he walked on towards the three huge back-up generators that stood encased in concrete, quietly waiting for something to go wrong. Seagulls wheeled overhead, their cracked cries echoing between the power station buildings.

Just after lunch, when no one was looking, Frank dropped an empty glass bottle onto the floor, then as he cleared it up he cut himself with one of the shards. Just enough to warrant a trip to the health clinic. Walking with his hand cradled in front of him, Frank felt a curious excitement at seeing Alice again. It was as if she was drawing him to her – a magnetic attraction. Her youth and her beauty pulled him in. And after all, hadn't they shared something quite unique that night? Something far beyond the experience of most other human beings.

Thankfully he'd timed it right. She was free. After a moment's hesitation and a glance around, Alice took him into a cubicle where she motioned to him to sit on the edge of a bed. On first seeing him her eyes had given a kick of recognition, though he couldn't tell what emotion lay underneath. For a long time they were both silent. She looked different. Her face was thinner and had lost its rosiness; indeed there was a sickly yellow tinge around her eyes.

She was shaking. And yet her eyes were not afraid of him.

'How are you?' he said as she dabbed antiseptic liquid onto his hand with a ball of cotton wool. In its smooth rubber protection, baby blue, her hand looked so delicate compared to his great chipolata fingers, browned by the summer and scored by age. By way of reply to his question, a single tear fell from her and splashed onto his wrist. When she straightened, the look on her face was defiant.

'How am I?' she said, trying to keep her voice down. 'How am I? Fucking hell.'

Though her physical appearance was diminished, her voice was as robust as he remembered it. There was steel in this girl.

'It is strange,' Frank said carefully, for he was conscious of playing to a gallery of unknown colleagues beyond the white screens. 'I just hope they find him soon.'

Releasing a bandage from its packet, she came close. He smelt the soap on her hands. Sensed the solidity of her young body, so much more vigorous than his fast-disintegrating own.

'What have you got to say to me?' she said at last. 'What?'

Frank smiled. 'What do I have to say to you? Well, you're safe, aren't you? So I say that I am glad you are safe.'

'Safe?' she hissed.

A shadow passed across the pale blue cubicle curtain, a figure walking back and forth. Frank looked down and saw a pair of scuffed black high heels.

Ungrateful bitch. Doesn't she understand what you did for her?

Oh, so you're back.

Just tell her.

'Alice, I did it for you. To protect you.'

Alice swung her hand up, slapping him a hard sting on the cheek. Then turned and tore open the curtain. There was no one else there as she walked away.

Frank wondered what he would ever have to do to please Andrea.

The rest of the afternoon passed slowly. For the most part he was absorbed in his work, but occasionally in a quiet moment he thought of her and wondered if she was developing feelings for him, and couldn't quite process the complexity of the situation. Hence the lashing out. It was common enough. A young girl saved by an older man. Protector becomes lover. It was all very flattering, but dangerous.

• • •

Maynard's car was found later that day. It pointed, the policeman told Judy, to the conclusion that Maynard was still in the area. You mean his body, said Judy. When Gail, who had been present for the policeman's visit, reported the discussion to Frank she added that Judy seemed unnaturally calm. The discovery of her husband's car at this remote spot, unlocked, with the keys in the ignition, caused her no surprise.

A search was organised for the following morning. Working with the Seton One management, the police split the sixty or so volunteers into groups of ten and, starting from the place where his car had been found, the groups were given directions by a grizzled police detective with a walking stick. Three groups were each allocated a section of the beach and dunes. The other three groups were pointed inland, given a compass and bearing and told to fan out.

Judy stayed at home, with Gail for company. Anthony joined the search but was put into a different group to Frank, who was relieved to find himself being pointed away from the beach. Not that he expected the search there to yield any results. His analysis of the tidal flow looked to have been correct; the police had done a cursory sweep of the beach when they found the car, and found nothing. The body had been taken out to sea and even if it did wash up somewhere eventually, it was highly unlikely to be back here. No, Frank just wanted to avoid the beach because...well, it was difficult to explain, even to himself. He just knew that the sand down there by the water's edge had such treacherous suction.

The police didn't really believe the search would turn anything up. It was a public relations exercise, and a way to show they were doing something, when in reality they were just waiting for some fisherman to find Maynard's body in his nets. The walking-stick detective barked orders at them and although he surely didn't believe they would find anything gruesome, the detective's eyes shone with a boyish excitement. As if he'd been waiting for this opportunity for years. A good old dead-body search. Perhaps he understood that the most enjoyable part of a dead-body search was the actual process of searching, the drama that comes of not knowing what will be under the next bush. The outcome wasn't such a big deal. Among the searchers, too, there were a few excited individuals. They asked all kinds of questions: 'What do we do if we find anything?' 'Can you give us more details of the case, you know, to help us search?' 'How do we secure the crime scene?'

Frank recognised a couple of his group as Seton One workers and introduced himself. If word got back to the plant that he'd been on the search that would help him. Given his friendship with Maynard it would have looked odd if he hadn't been there. They exchanged a few banalities about how terrible this all was, and how it was hard to know what kind of shoes to wear for this sort of thing, and set off. It was slow-going and futile work.

Into a field of barley, where the dusty soil subsided under every step and the crop scratched their legs. Most of the group had now found themselves a stick and were describing semi-circles as they walked, divining for Maynard's blood. Silence between them, gulls and rooks wheeling above, the wind moaning.

He imagined what they might look like from above, a line of black dots creeping across the fields. To the birds they were slow, lumbering and inconsequential. And from the ground? Huge crashing shadows of death. Could the animals detect his radiation? Did he, to them, glow? Or could they detect a buzz? He had no idea what level he was up to now, but he'd heard stories about American scientists on the Manhattan Project being buried deep in the desert in lead caskets, such was the threat their remains were deemed to pose.

No one really knew anything about radiation, of course. If they claimed to understand it, they were lying.

They'd been told to look for articles of clothing and possible weapons. That they were also looking for a body hadn't been stated explicitly, but was obvious. It was rather an effort for Frank to keep his head down when he knew there was no chance of finding anything. At the end of the first field they regrouped, took slugs of water from flasks, commented on how sad and tragic this all was. Any initial excitement at being involved in the search seemed to have faded, replaced by a realisation that finding anything was unlikely. Frank could have told them that.

They beat a path through a thicket and emerged into another barley field. As they neared the other side there was a scream. A woman, away to Frank's right, had stopped and was holding her hand up in the air, as she'd been taught. For a moment, the group stood motionless where they'd stopped, too stunned to react. Frank's mind, which had been getting dozy in the sunshine, whirred into life.

How was this possible? He'd left Maynard dead on the beach. Could it be that he'd actually been still alive and had somehow managed to crawl all this way? No, impossible. Then whose was this body?

He thrashed through the barley towards the woman. She was pointing with her stick and as he got closer he could see a dark form on the ground, partially obscured by the crops, a halo of flies in the air above.

Frank felt sickness rising in his throat but kept moving. He had to see the body. He went past the woman who was rooted to the spot and waved the flies away with his stick. On the ground lay the rotting body of a muntjac deer. Flesh ripped, blood sticky and gleaming in the sun, eyes swivelled in lunatic fear. The stench coming off it was putrid and insidious.

• • •

The next day, a Saturday, Frank was alone in the house when the doorbell rang. At first he didn't move from the armchair where he was sitting, newspaper on his lap, cup of tea and chocolate biscuits on the adjacent table. He wasn't expecting anyone. Gail could have lost or forgotten her keys – it wouldn't have been the first time – but she'd only just left for the hairdressers. No, he'd better go.

When he opened the door he found Judy standing square before him. She was wearing a long black dress that billowed around her body, a theatrical touch Frank quite appreciated. And her neck and cheeks were flushed, not from physical exertion, he guessed, but from anger. Her eyes were hard as stone and he could see she was trying not to cry.

'She's not here,' Frank said, but she gave a quick shake of her head and marched past him into the house.

'I know.'

He clicked the door shut and followed her scent into the kitchen.

'Oh Christ, I can't bear it, that fucking bitch,' she said, pacing around in a tight circle. 'My husband is missing, presumed dead, and she's telling me now that I'm doing my own daughter's hair wrong. I mean, who gives a fuck? Really, who fucking gives...'

The anger cut off any more words. Fists balled, she bent over double and let out a sound between a grunt and a yell, purging the rage from deep within her body. Now her whole face reddened and when she straightened afterwards there were tears trembling on her eyelashes.

'Sorry,' she said.

What would Gail say and do? In these sort of situations, Frank knew he was hopeless unless he tried to think how his wife would respond. It was dishonest really, because it meant any reaction wasn't his own but a poor simulation of someone with genuine empathy. Still, it made life easier.

'Sometimes you've got to let it all out. It's good for you,' Frank replied, looking around for a box of tissues.

'Mothers – who'd have them? I mean, God, it's so painful. Everything I do... I just had to get out of the house, I'm sorry. Do you have anything to drink?'

Frank poured them both a gin and tonic. Judy gulped two-thirds in one go.

'You were on the search, weren't you? What was it like? It's all right, you don't have to answer that. I can imagine – boring, appalling, hard work; ultimately pointless – right?'

'Pretty much.'

'They're just waiting for him to wash up on a beach somewhere.'

'No...you don't know that. He'll turn up... I mean, alive.'

She shook her head, pulled a chair out from under the kitchen table and sat down. He did likewise.

'I'm not surprised, you know,' she said.

'At what?' Frank was intrigued, and a little worried, about where this conversation was going. He didn't feel prepared to talk to Judy, to sit just a few inches from her, just the two of them in the warm airless room, enveloped in the buzz of the fridge and the energy of their bodies. She sat slumped in the chair. He thought about when they'd danced together. That night seemed a long, long time ago.

'That he's done this. Taken this way out. He always seems so strong and bullish; optimistic, right? But that's all a cover. Just an act, really. Underneath he's fragile. I'm the strong one. I'm the one talking him round. Typical bloody man. My father was the same. We always wondered why he'd spend so much time in bed. Only later when we were grown up did we realise it was because he had these black moods – couldn't do anything other than stay in bed all day.'

'Does anyone else know? About Maynard, I mean.'

'I've told the police. That's why they didn't expand the search. They suspected it anyway. People don't just go missing and leave their car like that. If he'd run off with some dolly bird, like that tart from the health clinic, he would have taken the car, emptied the bank account, packed his bloody rugby kit.'

Alarmed at the mention of Alice, Frank ventured, 'Tart from the health clinic? Who do you mean?'

Judy fixed him with an excoriating look. 'Don't be silly Frank, we're all grown-ups. You know what I'm talking about. I'm not going to say her name.'

'As far as I know nothing happened between them.'

'That's hardly the point is it?'

They fell silent.

So Gail would know about Alice too, given Judy's propensity for candour.

'Frank. You're a good man. I can see that. You've got integrity. You know who you are. But you've made one mistake.'

He felt the breath rush out of his lungs. She knew. She knew. Like the merman she could see the truth deep in him.

She went on, 'You haven't given your wife a child. She so desperately wants a baby. I can't explain to you what it means to a woman. But...well, just get on with it. Don't keep her waiting. And while I'm dishing out advice, go and see a doctor – you look absolutely terrible. You're working too hard. It's that place – it puts such a burden on you all. Maynard couldn't cope with it either. If nothing else I want people to learn from this. That place is brutal.'

With a sigh that seemed to express all that she had been through, and all that she was still to face, Judy rose from her chair. After he'd shown her out, Frank walked around the house, opening and closing his fists, trying to fight off the memories of Maynard's skull shattering under his blows, finding that images of the boy in the pub came to him too, the blood that clung to Frank's knuckles with every punch. He would drive back to the river where he'd thrown the bloodied jack and take it to the police. Offer his fingerprints and a confession. I killed Maynard Scott.

Frank went into the bedroom. As he walked around the bed, in the periphery of his vision he saw a figure standing in the centre of the back garden. It was the woman in the green dress. Andrea. No movement in her, other than the wind tugging at her hair.

He went through the kitchen to the back door. The plastic handle was slippery in his fingers. The glass in the door was mottled so he couldn't see whether she was still there in the garden. Turning the handle, he drew a breath and pushed the door.

She was right there at the door, a foot away, her demonic face looming. Her arm went up and he saw the blade gleaming in the sunlight. He sank to his knees, unable to resist, all strength seeping out of his body. But no blow came. When he looked up next, her hand was by her side and he couldn't see a blade. She was laughing at him. Still laughing, she squatted in front of him and put a finger under his chin. Her face was gaunt, brackish. Her eyes were hatched with black lines. Not so quick, they said.

22

ROTATION

Meet me in H5 at 10, by the ponds. Alice's handwriting was childishly neat and bubbly. It was five to ten now. Frank glanced through the other post in his pigeonhole, tucked the smaller letters inside his jacket, and turned up the collar of his mackintosh. After so many weeks of heat and light, to wake this morning to a steady soft rain was odd. Gail, in bed beside him, her body so rich and warm, had gasped with delight. And the landscape, too, seemed relieved to have this freshening downfall. Under the relentless sun of recent weeks the meadows had become yellow as cornfields, the streams dwindled, hedgerows sagged.

Because the site was so windy, carrying an umbrella around Seton One was not advised. In weather such as this most members of staff had heavy raincoats and a variety of hats. Some even had sou'westers borrowed from friendly fishing crews. Frank had a tweed flat cap, the peak of which he now held on to as he rounded the turbine building and crossed into the red zone. Somewhere an alarm bell was ringing. There were very few people about. It often seemed that the station was running itself. Perhaps in the future that would be the case. The control room, the impenetrable brain of the operation, could surely be automated. Computers could make the decisions. The robots could move uranium about, analyse the fuel rods, repair the turbines.

Climbing the metal stairs that ran in a zig-zag up the side of H5, Frank tried to calculate the best way to let Alice down. He wasn't interested in having an affair with her. Not that he didn't find her attractive, but...well, he loved Gail, and he didn't need anyone else. It was natural enough for the protected to fall for the protector, but Alice had to understand that he had not acted with the aim of getting into her bed. That would make him no better than Maynard. At the top of the stairs he paused to catch his breath; it felt like a flame had been lit inside his lungs. From up there, five flights up, he could see over the perimeter fence, past the flood defence banks and out to sea. The rain had turned all into rumpled, soft grey cloth.

Frank opened the heavy door of H5, a cavernous shed that contained three cooling ponds, and stepped inside.

Pond was a misleadingly pastoral name for what were essentially huge rectangular tanks of water. In each pond was a quantity of radioactive waste, mainly spent fuel rods, but also any piece of metalwork that had been extracted from the reactor core. As long as it was submerged the material was safe. If the tanks were drained and the material exposed to air it was so buzzy that it would heat up and quickly start a fire. H5 was an important building but no one worked there other than twice-daily inspections at noon and midnight. Devices monitored the water levels and triggered alarms if they detected a drop. It was a peaceful sort of place, if you could come to terms with the critical threat of what lay beneath. The water, motionless, gave no sound yet it was reassuring, a natural element in a contrived world.

Frank's boots clanged on the metal gangway running alongside the first tank. The water shimmered blue-green under the strip lights in the ceiling. Jumbled together on the floor, under twenty feet of water, were piles of grey material. An untouchable miniature Atlantis. The stuff down there would go on being highly radioactive for thousands of years. No one had the slightest idea what to do with it next.

Alice was standing on a wide concrete walkway between two tanks. She was wearing a man's raincoat, far too big for her, and a wide-brimmed sun hat with a red ribbon. If it hadn't been for the look on her face, Frank would have laughed at her.

Frank recalibrated. So she hadn't invited him here because she wanted him. Well, that was all right. In fact, that was good, wasn't it? Frank didn't want Alice to feel afraid of him, but some emotional distance between them was probably a good thing.

She'd been crying. She looked so delicate, but really was tough. Perhaps he'd misjudged her. Perhaps she could have rescued herself from Maynard's foul intentions. Before either of them could say anything, the door that

Frank had come in through clanged, letting in a gust of wind.

Alice glanced at the banging door but plainly did not see the ghost who entered through it and was now breathing on Frank's neck. He stiffened but forced himself to stay put. Today Andrea was watchful and silent, and ever stronger. The radiation made her stronger just as it did him.

Alice said, 'I'm not scared of you, you know.'

She's testing you, just testing you. She doesn't know anything.

'You have no need to be scared of me, I came to rescue you. To look after you. That still applies.'

Andrea growled at his admission. Her fingers took hold of his wrists and squeezed. Alice flinched, as if his words caused her physical pain.

'How did you get home, that night?' he asked, but Alice ignored him.

'Where is he?' Alice said. 'Where? I mean, people can't just disappear.'

'The less you know the better.'

Now she came closer and spat the words at him. 'For fuck's sake, Frank. What's the matter with you? Don't you understand? You're...you're behaving like it's some perfectly normal little science experiment.'

'Alice, it was self-defence, he came at me with a weapon. I had to defend myself.'

She staggered backwards, her face reddening as tears filled her eyes, mouth slack, fists balled. Shook her head.

'No, no, I don't believe you. He told me about what you did to that boy in Oxford.'

'No, that was different, totally different. I was looking

after you.'

'I don't need looking after, you nut-job. I can look after myself.'

Frank jerked his head towards the sea. 'The sea took him.'

'Then the sea will give him back. You don't understand the currents off these beaches, do you? He's coming back.' She stepped backwards.

Frank shook his head.

'He's coming back for you, Frank.'

Don't listen to her. She's empty, worthless.

Alice seemed on the brink of saying something else, her prepared nerve having melted into a look almost of tenderness towards him. But the words did not come and she turned away.

• • •

Alice knew that even if someone did come to ask her about what happened that night, her credibility as a witness was sketchy. She hadn't seen Frank clearly and she didn't know what happened between the two men after she ran off. For all she knew Maynard may well have come at Frank with a weapon.

She had, however, achieved her main purpose – to get Frank to admit what she already knew, that it was him on the beach that night. He had killed Maynard. And not a flicker of remorse in his eyes. He really seemed to believe that he'd been saving her from...from what? Rape? Having sex with someone he didn't like? That was it: simple male jealousy. Frank didn't like Maynard and didn't want him to get his end away.

Oh God, what a mess.

With trembling hands she lit a cigarette and crouched down on her haunches, her back to the wall of H5. The staircase above her partly shielded her from the rain. She tried to think.

He'd followed them there. That meant it was premeditated. Or maybe not; he may only have planned to confront them about the affair. What a self-righteous dick!

The dazzling glare of his headlights.

Maynard had nothing in the car that could constitute a weapon. Not that she'd seen, anyway.

Run, he'd called. Not *Run, Alice*. If he'd said her name it would prove that he knew who was there in front of him.

The sea took him. The sea took him. So he was out there somewhere, poor sod – what was left of him, anyway. And he would come back, she was sure of that. Most likely a few miles down the coast. Fall off a trawler out to sea and you'd never be seen again, but within five hundred yards of the beach the looping currents brought objects, and bodies, back to the coast.

Those poor kids. And his wife, what hell was she going through?

The powerful toxin of guilt rushed in. Alice saw the whole business with new detachment, She'd gone with him out there, she'd seduced him. And at the same time she must have given the impression to Frank that she needed salvation. If it wasn't for her, Maynard would be alive today.

She'd led him to his death.

And yet no one other than Frank seemed to know

about their affair. No policeman had come knocking on her door (thank God) to ask about her relationship with the missing party. Even if Judy suspected something, either she didn't have enough evidence to implicate Alice, or she'd discounted Alice being involved.

So what was there to do, other than wait? As a little girl her father had told her stories – his own versions of the old tales, about monsters climbing out of the deep sea trenches, about mermen crawling onto the beaches at night and Lord Seton himself, pale and scaly, all his fury set on revenge.

Revenge, Maynard would want revenge. He wasn't the sort of man to rise above it. And if he couldn't come back in person to haunt his murderers, wouldn't he want someone to do it for him?

23

ELECTRICITY

Gail stood staring at the telephone, unable to pick it up. For so long she'd thought about this moment. Yet now it had come, she was gripped in a kind of stasis, suspended by…by what? She should be happy. This was going to be one of the moments of her life to savour. Three simple words to tumble down the wire to her mother's ear. I am pregnant. In her pre-visions of this moment, Frank had always been standing behind her, one hand protectively on her shoulder or even on her tummy. A faint, newly mature smile on his lips. But Frank wasn't with her. He was at work. He knew nothing about it because she couldn't bring herself to tell him, and surely that was not good in itself and…oh fuck.

This was it. This was the moment she had to go it

alone. All those nights she'd lain awake wondering if she had the guts to do it – to leave Frank, to bring up their child alone. Now she had to make a decision. Though hadn't he already made the decision for her?

With a stark clarity, she remembered that night. For a few moments the sex had been tender, even loving. Which made it even worse; it reminded her of the man he had once been. But afterwards that mask descended again. He left the room, naked, without a word, and she lay sobbing on the bed, holding her legs in the air as Joanne had told her. Swim little ones, oh please swim.

Gail's sister Joanne lived in a large house in Surrey with her three kids and her adorable husband, who not only earned a fortune but also cooked a lovely roast dinner. She had outbuildings, she did voluntary work at a local charity. A few years ago she'd had an affair and got away with it. When, after a few too many gins, she'd told Gail about it, there had been such a sneering self-satisfaction on her face, Gail had wanted to slap her.

Gail had always felt like a failure compared to Joanne, and this was supposed to be the moment things got evened out. For all her money and worrying about status, Joanne was a fiercely loving mother. Her children were everything to her. News of Gail's pregnancy would be met with delight, Gail knew that, and she felt guilty for thinking about her news as some kind of competitive initiative. Still, she couldn't help how she felt, could she?

She ran a finger down the telephone, then turned away and walked into the kitchen. How could it be that she was about to tell her mother before her husband? What wrong turn had she made in life to bring her here?

She sat down and lit a cigarette. The room began to

rotate, all its component parts shaking loose of each other. He did it. A whistling filled the space, becoming a roar. He did it. She pressed her palms into her eyes to stem the tears, put her feet flat and wide on the floor so as not to fall. He did it and she couldn't tell him about the baby. Anyone but him.

There was a seed growing inside her, changing her, glowing with life. Another human being. And she'd never felt so alone.

24

LEAKS

The next morning there was a memo in his pigeonhole asking him to report to Mr Parker's office at 11 o'clock. A bout of intense nausea meant he didn't fancy his usual chocolate biscuits at morning tea-break, so Frank just sipped a cup of scalding black tea from the canteen, sitting alone by a window and watching the pedestrian traffic outside. Engineers in blue coveralls, chemists like him in white coats, administrators, security guards, cleaners. A dehumanising place, the power station. If you worked here you were no more than your job. Everything had a process. That clarity of purpose and its attendant straightforwardness had once appealed to him. Now he could see through it. How many of these human bodies walking past his window were wracked by heavy drinking or drugs? How many minds were on the verge of breakdown? How many marriages were falling apart? Inhumane places broke lives.

Parker appeared not to have moved from his desk during the two-month interval since their little chat on Frank's first day. The same grey flannel suit, the same shock of white hair, and the same moaning about his arthritic knees. While Parker began talking about nothing in particular, Frank constructed a more meaningful interrogation in his head.

Mr Banner, why did you kill Mr Scott?

I didn't like him.

That's all? It doesn't seem a good enough reason for murder.

No one expects me to do anything bold.

You attacked that boy. Was that the same? Just attention-seeking?

Not attention-seeking. It's different.

How so?

Well, what would any of us do, if no one else were paying attention?

I don't subscribe to that. I think this is something else. Something unique to you. Something in your past, buried deep that forces this anger up through you.

You can think what you fucking well like, my friend. I just didn't like him.

Tuning back in, Frank found that Mr Parker was talking about cricket. It was a game Frank had never totally understood. And as if sensing his interviewee's ambivalence, the older man abruptly changed the subject.

'Frank, thank you for coming to see me. I'm just a little bit worried about what I hear. Three accidents in one month, all involving radiation leaks, and now this flask smashing. It's rather a lot, isn't it?'

'Just bad luck,' Frank said.

'Frank, your levels are off the scale. I should be taking you off front-line work but I just haven't got enough men with your skills, and production... Well, we've just got to keep on top of it. I am worried though. With levels like yours, well, I can overlook it this once, but beyond that we'll be in trouble.'

Frank took a packet of cigarettes out of his shirt pocket, offered one to Parker, who declined, then lit one for himself. He sat there for a while, blowing smoke sideways. Parker watched him with a slight frown. He had probably been expecting some kind of apology or excuse, or for Frank to blame others.

'When you first started working with radioactive materials, can you remember how they made you feel?' Frank said.

The frown deepened. 'How they made me feel?'

Frank nodded. 'And don't tell me you're a scientist and that you only deal in facts and processes and all that.'

Parker shifted in his seat, gazed briefly at the wall beyond Frank's head.

'Well, I was fascinated, I suppose. Still am. It's rather wonderful to think of that hidden world, that only we can see. And I've always believed in its power. One day the coal mines will stand empty and there'll dozens of power stations like this all around the country.'

Frank made a gesture with his cigarette to sweep away this public relations rhetoric.

'Of course, but when you were in the lab, not stuck in an office? When you handled the stuff? You weren't thinking about the future of British power generation then, presumably?'

Parker frowned. Was that too long ago for him to remember?

'I don't follow, Frank, I'm afraid.'

'We know nothing about what radiation actually does to our bodies, do we?'

'We know something. They used to think it was harmless. They used to sell it as a health tonic, you know. Then there were some unpleasant cases. I'm sure you know this?'

Parker's tone was condescending, and his expression worried. I shouldn't need to tell one of my top technicians this kind of stuff – that's what he's thinking, thought Frank. Time to switch the conversation. Parker's response was standard, unimaginative. He was a company man to the core. Beholden to Science and the Authority.

'Maynard was scared,' Frank said. Parker's face seemed to contract, to draw back from the implications of this statement.

'Of contamination?'

'He found a box of metal rods, down in P25. Turns out they were buzzing. He was supposed to go to the clinic but he ducked out of it. Said it wasn't a big deal.'

Parker took a moment to consider this question. 'The incident wasn't reported?'

'I have no idea. Anyway the point is that it frightened Maynard. He was worried about going home to his children, you know, still buzzing. I think the idea of radiation can do funny things to a man's mind. That is more dangerous than the actual stuff.'

'You're saying he was so scared he took his own life?'

Frank shrugged, took a long drag on his cigarette to buy time to think. He only wanted to plant ideas in the man's head, not prove anything.

'I don't know,' he said, after exhaling. 'I think he had other problems. Periods of darkness, feeling low. His wife said as much to me. I was surprised, but I suppose often the most robust-seeming men can hide it well.'

'There was a complaint against him,' Parker said quickly, leaning forward on his elbows, his eyes burning with a secret he wanted to divulge. 'Here, a formal complaint. But it really is confidential so you mustn't mention it. I've told the police of course.'

'What kind of complaint?' The old boy seemed to live vicariously through other people's secrets. He was himself a desiccated shell of a man, probably bullied by his wife, bored by every aspect of his job other than this – juicy memos about his staff.

'From a woman, in the administration building. Says he's been harassing her. Unwanted attention, that sort of thing. I must say he has something of a reputation for it around the site. I don't want to speak ill of the dead, but he really was a bit of a shit.'

Frank wondered if Judy knew. Probably not. It wasn't exactly the kind of thing one told one's wife. As if he knew what Frank was thinking, Parker asked how she was doing.

'Putting a brave face on it, I suppose you might say. With the help of the doctor and a lot of pills. My wife is helping with the children, and she's got family around her.'

'Has she said much about…about what might have driven him to do it?' asked Parker, and underneath the oh-so-gentle compassion Frank saw the steel of the man. So this was why he'd been summoned – to advise Parker whether Judy was going to cause him a problem. Of course, Parker wanted to avoid the power station being dragged into this. Either Maynard's recent contamination or this complaint against him could be seen as reasons for his suicide. Parker's job was safety, productivity and public relations, but not necessarily in that order.

Frank selected his words carefully, wondering whether to try to draw Parker out, or just end the conversation and get out of the bloody room. 'Well, like I said, the depression, that's all she has said. To me, anyway.'

There was a moment's silence while Parker digested the meaning of this last comment. Women talk to women. Judy would tell Gail, not him.

'Frank, you're a good man. I value your contribution here. You understand how important it is that people don't jump to the wrong conclusions. You're close to the family. Anything you can do to manage the situation, even if it's just coming for a quick chat with me every once in a while, would be most welcome. I think we can do great work together, important work for the future, and your role in it can be central. But first we need to eradicate any distractions.'

The devious old fucker. Inform on poor Judy and in return a promise, though vague, of a better job. The self-preservation instinct had taken over in Parker; perhaps he'd already had calls from the newspapers, and from the Authority. Frank could just imagine him taking the call from London, obsequiously promising to make the whole thing go away. Suicide was shameful. And if the complaint against Maynard had tipped him over the edge, well, that would be very awkward indeed.

Other men would see an opportunity in this, thought Frank as he walked back to the lab – a way to secure a better job by doing what the old bastard wanted. But not me. I'm working to higher standards here.

The wind came riffling around the buildings and, riding it, she whispered, *The girl, the girl –she'll trip you up; she's a clever one – too clever.*

Yes I know, he muttered, I know. He patted his breast pocket. Inside was a small tin containing two ounces of uranium-235.

25

WASTE

Cold, wet and very dead. Two dozen lunatic eyeballs staring up at the white tiled ceiling. Cod, haddock, plaice, sprats – all kinds. The sparkle of sunlight refracted through the plate-glass window and onto a bank of ice cubes. Purple stains on the fishmonger's tunic. Gail had been standing in a queue for ten minutes and every time she shuffled closer to the front, she felt a little sicker. Her mission, and it was beginning to feel like one, was just to buy a fish for her and baby's dinner. Brain food, didn't they say that? Start as you mean to go on and all that. But could she get to the front, select a fish and pay for it before vomiting all over this shiny floor?

'Haddock, please.'

'Haddock, madam, absolutely. How many?'

'Two please, and erm...what would be a good thing to have with the fish?'

'To have with the haddock? For dinner, you mean? Well, I'd say potatoes. Boiled potatoes.'

It didn't sound very imaginative to Gail, but she didn't argue. The fishmonger was known to be against Seton One and nuclear power generally, and had a large knife in his hand. Holding the cool, fat package, Gail dived out into the fresh air, just managing to keep her breakfast down.

She walked a little way down the high street, trying to breathe, telling herself that this was all perfectly normal, and good; it was all good. Yet why did she feel on the verge of tears?

The sun was pitiless on her head, on her bare shoulders. She longed for rain and a cool morning. The days passed so slowly, agonisingly so, and yet time was against her – soon she'd have to tell Frank. It was only because he was so distracted that he hadn't put it together himself. Being sick every morning wasn't normal, but then he was quite often sick in the mornings too. It was radiation sickness; she knew it.

A tap on her shoulder. Gail turned and found Alice standing there. The girl looked pale and dishevelled, with big dark rings around her eyes.

'You look how I feel,' said Gail.

'Well, I feel like shit.'

'That sounds about right. Are you busy right now? I mean, can I buy you a drink?'

Alice nodded. She'd lost something: her usual coolness, her relaxed energy. As she walked her frame was hunched forward and she stared at the ground, her hair hanging limply across her face. They went to the Wheatsheaf to avoid fishermen and scientists.

'It's awful about Maynard, isn't it?' said Gail once they'd settled on a table in a quiet, dingy corner.

Alice had been gazing into her drink, and now, when she raised her eyes to Gail's, the older woman saw just how wracked with misery they were. Alice said, 'How are Judy and the kids?'

'The kids don't really understand. Judy's a mess, as you'd expect.'

Alice bit her lip. She had a bar mat in her fingers and was picking at it.

Gail lowered her voice. 'Alice, do you know something about it?'

The girl shook her head.

'Alice…'

The stony expression dissolved and when the tears came they tumbled from her. She sobbed silently into a man's handkerchief that she'd pulled from her pocket.

'Alice, this is between us only. I won't tell anyone. You can tell me. God knows, who would I tell?'

At this last comment, Alice looked up at Gail through the prism of the tears trembling on her eyelashes.

Maynard was dead. Gail knew that. Everyone knew that. Did it really matter how it happened? Gail felt gripped by a sudden clarity, exhilarating in its iciness. The living matter – and her baby more than anything else. She had to focus on her priorities. Fuck Maynard, and fuck Frank.

'I was there. I saw it.'

'Saw what?'

'That's just it, I don't really know.'

So Alice told Gail the whole story. And Gail tried not to react, tried to hide her abject terror. Since Maynard's disappearance every kind of scenario had played through her mind, all involving her husband. Some, in which Maynard had suffered an accidental death for which Frank couldn't be blamed, had felt sugary and fanciful. Horribly, it was the darker versions that felt most real. What Alice told her wasn't the full picture, she was sure of that, but it allowed room for that darkness.

'And this attacker, you have no idea who it was?' Gail said, trying to keep her voice neutral.

Alice shook her head. 'It all happened so fast, and it was dark and... I was so scared, I just ran.'

'All right, it's all right,' Gail whispered, taking Alice's hand. 'I won't say a word to anyone.'

'We should go to the police,' Alice said, now defiant. She's testing me, thought Gail.

'It would look a bit odd, wouldn't it? Going to the police now? If they asked you why you hadn't gone before, what would you say?'

'He shouldn't be allowed to get away with it. He's a monster.'

'But you don't even know who it is. Or what really happened. Besides the police know someone else is involved, so what would you really be adding to the picture, Alice? Just yourself, you'd be putting yourself in there, and that could cost you a great deal. Think of the effect on your family, and on Judy. It's better you stay out of it, believe me.'

'They know there was someone else involved?'

'They told Judy,' Gail lied. 'I'm not supposed to know. Trust me, it will sort itself out.'

Gail squeezed Alice's hand and the girl winced as Gail's wedding ring dug into her skin.

• • •

These fucking outsiders...coming here and messing with us... What right did they have? She'd been a fool to think that she could become one of them.

Leaving Gail in the pub, Alice walked along the harbour wall, looking down into the oily water. Gail was pregnant; that much was obvious. Too much holding of her belly. God help her with Frank for a husband. She knew, too. Alice was sure of that. Her eyes had been full of fear, and all that desperate persuasion of Alice not to go to the police. Gail needn't have worried. There was no point in going to the police. Alice had faith that some other power, more pervasive, more penetrating, would put this situation right. Frank wasn't going to get away with it.

She slipped between two fisherman's huts, and turning into the narrow lane that ran down past the Methodist chapel, she felt that she was being watched. Not stopping, she glanced over her shoulder but saw no one. Walking a little faster now, she thought she heard a foot crunch on stones. Turned again and this time saw a figure tucked into the shadow of a tall house. A man, not moving, about two hundred yards back. There was no one else around.

For a moment, neither of them moved. She couldn't see him well, but she knew it was Frank. Part of her wanted to call his name out, to stride down towards him and demand he explain himself. But the street was too empty, and the gulls croaking overhead sounded like harbingers of death, and she imagined him producing a knife from his jacket, those uncomprehending eyes of his as he pushed her to the floor. And again the coward won. She ran to the nearest alleyway and sprinted breathlessly towards the safety of the high street.

26

CONTAMINATION

The wind blew sand across his face. He wasn't far from her shack now. A small red car purred past him and disappeared around a shimmering bend in the road.

After a day spent in rooms with no windows, with constant alarms and safety announcements, the odour of cleaning fluids, the discomfort of protective clothing, to cycle along the beach road was a salve to his frazzled head. This place seemed to exist in two very separate dimensions: the misty horizon, with its abstract striations of sky and sea, and the visceral tarmac melting beneath his tyres.

He was going to her for sanctuary. Only she could give him hope. The sight of Gail and Alice talking in the pub (he'd followed Alice from her house, seen her bump into

Gail and followed them both there, where he'd concealed himself in the lounge bar behind a newspaper) had been a shock. What had that girl said? Had she told Gail that she knew he was there that night? That she'd given him an ultimatum to give himself up? This was a valuable lesson indeed – the saved cannot always make the right judgments. They cannot see what's been done in their name.

Of course Andrea had been vehement in her damnations. He was getting used to that now. But he wasn't owned by her. He was his own man. When the cosy little chat ended, he'd followed Alice across the harbour and down the lane that stank of fish guts and beer, and she'd felt his presence, turning round just when there was nowhere for him to hide. Not so brave now, without her beefy security detail, she'd turned and run down an alleyway. He let her go; after all, he had no intention of doing her harm. But he was very disappointed. That she'd told his wife their secret wasn't something that could be ignored.

Chest heaving from the exertion of pedalling the old bike against the wind, Frank came to a stop at the familiar place. But when he looked towards the dunes he couldn't see the pebbles that had lined her path. He dropped the bike and, wiping his brow with his shirt-sleeve, stepped into the sand. No pebbles, but he could see the corner of the shack poking out from behind the dune. God he just wanted to sit with her and rest his head. Not talk, not think, just rest. He was so tired.

Every step revealed more of the shack and his body convulsed in horror as he saw the delicate plumes of smoke rising, the charred wood, the shimmer of heat in the air. The fire was over but not by long. Being wooden, and dry as anything after such a summer, the building would have gone up quickly. Now it was nothing but a black cave emitting an evil acrid stench, its structure undermined. Surely it would collapse in on itself any moment. There was no sign of her motorbike, her easels or paintings, or any other personal items. Coolly he wondered if she was inside, but felt instinctively that she was not. He followed the curling smoke up into the white sky.

He backed away from the smouldering shack. The light, the cavernous sea, the pitiless sand, all pressed on him. An image of Maynard's smashed face struck him like a bird striking a window. The crazed absence that death entailed. The vacuum into which he'd pushed a man. And his remains out there somewhere, nibbled by fish, bandaged in seaweed.

Frank looked south along the beach, expecting to see Maynard crawl out of the waves but instead he saw another figure in the distance. It was her. Her shape, her size. She was waving, then putting her hand to her mouth to call out but she was too far away. He couldn't hear. He walked, then ran, towards her. But with every step of his, she seemed to move further away, become less distinct. The beach dissolved into a white haze around her, swirled across her face. His lungs and legs gripped by pain, Frank came to a stop and sank to his knees. He was alone now. Utterly alone. He watched her slide away into nothingness and was overcome with the terror of abject isolation. And if he followed his mother into that nothingness, would anyone notice or care?

But of course he was not alone. Andrea was there at his shoulder, a hoarse whisper, a scent on the wind.

They've all left you, she spat at him now, so *get up. Act like a man. I'm all you've got left. No wife, no mother, no friends. Just me.*

With no refuge, no protection from her, he was more afraid than ever. Her malice was laced with insanity. She craved blood and destruction. And how could he get away from her?

He began to run, as if she were physical, all the while knowing it was hopeless. She just laughed in his ear. He stopped and slammed his fists into the sides of his head; perhaps he could knock her out of there. But no blow would do that. He recited a few lines of a prayer his mother had taught him. Again Andrea laughed.

We are bound, you and I, she said. *Now go home and rest.*

27

NAUSEA

The sickness was getting worse. And what had been aches in his bones were now sharpening into excruciating pains. It was becoming hard to hide his reactions to them. At work he'd constructed an elaborate history of sporting injuries to explain why he kept wincing and yelping. On top of all that, over the last few days whenever he took a shit, the toilet bowl was crimson with blood. Not a good sign. It was, of course, the radiation. By his own reckoning, he'd had two sieverts over the past six weeks. It was moving through him, scouring and slicing and scraping. He was becoming stronger. At good moments he felt invincible. Energy crackled through him, he would not have been astonished to see electric currents fly from his fingers. These aches and pains were, in the greater scheme of things, trivial. Growing pains; that was all.

Gail was still talking, but he was no longer listening. He'd heard enough of her pathetic justifications. Why couldn't she just be fucking honest? Why couldn't she say, I'm leaving you because I think you're a murderer? Simple. But no, she had to tie herself up in these linguistic knots, always hesitating and modifying. It was cowardly and he hated her for it. She understood nothing about what he'd become. It didn't matter. The hero has a lonely path.

She was red-cheeked and strands of hair stuck to the side of her face. Her eyes were bloodshot and she sat with her feet well apart, as if the baby could drop out any time. The kitchen clock ticked away. The last slants of evening sunshine were slowly thinning.

This is necessary, that familiar voice whispered, *necessary for you and me to be alone. To get on with things. She's a useless distraction.*

I won't touch her, Frank thought, I will not touch her. I used, once, to love her. Though it seemed like a thousand years ago, he remembered that feeling, the warmth it gave him. Of course, since then he'd chosen another way. Gail could not be expected to understand, and it was impossible to explain. Better just to let her and the boy (for Andrea had told him the baby was a boy) go.

Put the poor cow out of her misery. Get rid of her tonight.

After these words he felt Andrea's presence fade away. She was his angel now, blackened and hard as she was. Since the beach their relationship had been sure. He put his forefinger up to his cheek and traced his scar. It was her mark on him, reassuring and soft.

Gail had stopped talking now and was gazing at him with trembling, tear-laden eyes. He nodded to show he understood what she was saying.

'Will you do something for me?' Frank said eventually.

'What?'

'Send me pictures of him. Once a year, on his birthday.'

She sobbed then as he'd never seen before, letting out a cry that cut straight through him, nearly reanimating that part of him that might have saved him. And yet even his wife's utter despair could not touch him now. He was a radioactive being, a hidden force, good only for revenge, not love.

28

FEAR

When he returned to Fisher Close it was growing dark. The house was empty. Gail had gone. Probably to her sister's house; she'd taken the car. Otherwise the house seemed unchanged, same sink full of dirty dishes, same lipstick-streaked cigarette butts in the ashtray, same faint brown smear on the kitchen wall where she'd thrown a cup of coffee at him the day before her Big Decision. It was laughable, the energy she'd wasted on the whole business. All that crying and wailing. Stupid bitch. She knew her mind, knew what she was going to do. So why all the emotion? Leaving one's husband, just like marrying the poor bastard, was a process. Keep it simple. Inefficiency can never be excused.

Walking from room to room he began to notice the

space where she had taken things. A framed photograph, her make-up and hairbrushes, the book from her bedside table. He felt nothing about this. Nothing at all.

Later, he lay in bed, trying to reason with Andrea.

But the girl is innocent.

Ungrateful, spoilt, vindictive. She's laughing at you. She thinks she can get one over on you, and you've given her the ammunition haven't you? Admitted your guilt.

She won't go to the police.

Doesn't need to, does she? All she needs to do is breathe your name and the rumour will start. Won't be long before the police pick it up.

I just can't do it, don't you understand?

No, Frank, don't you understand? You're mine now. I'm all you have. I won't watch them put you away. We have too much ahead of us. The future, Frank. Think of the future.

He felt her in bed with him, rustling through the sheets, sliding across his skin. Her knees pressing on his chest and the blade cutting his skin. The soft fabric of the green dress, now dirtied and creased. The floral perfume failing to mask the sour odour of death.

Who are you?

Life's been mean to me. I've only got bitterness left. You can rely on pain, it's a lot easier to find than happiness.

Is that why you're haunting me, because I ruined your life?

You, ruin my life? Ha! Your little episode with my boy was nothing compared to what I've been through. And with all I've been through, and put others through, it was inevitable I'd end up here.

In prison?

Is that where you think I am? Oh no, I'm here with you aren't I? And I'm nowhere. My body is lying in a mortuary in Oxford, only a few floors down from where you were sewn up by those clever doctors. How often I thought of creeping into that hospital ward and ripping your face open again. That thought kept me going all through the trial. Only when they put me into the cell and turned that key – oh the sound of it – only then did I know it was all over.

Her fingertips stroked his face, then encircled his throat, but he did not resist. Though those fingers were cold, her body was warm. He held the corrugations of her ribcage, seized the sharp hip-bone, sank into her defeated flesh.

Frank left the house at five o'clock in the morning and cycled along the coast road as the first mists of dawn rose from the horizon. Too early for any of his neighbours to be up, too early even for the milkman. It felt good to be out of that blasted house. Away from her (well, perhaps not away – he would never really get away – but at least away from the smell and the feel of her, and that prison of a bedroom). He had dozed fitfully, jerked awake often, sweating, burning, nauseous. Now the sea air could cleanse him. After all, he was pure in purpose. He knew what he had to do to survive. Andrea was right. The girl had pushed him too far. And in telling Gail, she'd deprived him of the one chance he had for redemption. Oh yes, Andrea had been quite clear on that; *I'm no angel*, she'd said, *only a partner. The only person who could have saved you has just walked out of the door with your son in her belly. And who told her that you were a killer?*

• • •

Alice never saw Maynard in her dreams. Not directly anyway. Thank fuck.

Yet she frequently dreamt of the sea, of being submerged, of opening her mouth to scream and having salt water fill her lungs, and she'd wake gulping, her legs kicking in spasms. After that a satisfying sleep was impossible, and she was too tired to read, so she just lay with her eyes heavy, listening to the sea. Grief (if that's what it was) was so tiring. She made more and more mistakes at work. Colleagues commented on the bags under her eyes, assumed she'd been out drinking.

On this particular morning she hadn't dreamt of the sea but woke early anyway, and found that she could think clearly enough to consider future plans. She felt somehow different to previous days, more clear-headed. And her first thought was: I will leave this place. This cannot defeat me.

In fact, didn't it give her more incentive to get away? If she stayed she'd be haunted for the rest of her life. She'd been a fool to think attaching herself to a man was the way to do it. Fuck men. Fuck making yourself an accessory. No, there had to be ways to do it alone. Perhaps she would go and speak to Parker, tell him what she wanted and see what happened. Didn't he have a daughter her age? *She* was probably at university but then Alice could have been too if she hadn't... Oh well, that was all old ground. No point in looking back.

But she felt guilty for having a future. Maynard didn't, poor sod. She remembered holding hands with him, like teenage lovers, her fingers so white and smooth against his dark and gnarled paw. His dull gold wedding band cut into the flesh of his ring finger. When he wasn't paying attention she ran the tip of her own finger along the band.

Fuck, she'd thought, I'm never getting married.

• • •

The father was the first to leave the house, a hunched figure in a long brown coat. The family dog bumped into his legs as his master paused to light a cigarette, then the pair of them headed away from the village. The boatyard was half a mile away, marooned on an expanse of shingle. Frank had cycled past it once.

Sitting on a damp upturned wooden crate, in the shadow of a trawler, Frank was not feeling good. Though the sun would surely begin to warm the land soon, at this hour the cold was surprising and insidious. He was under-dressed for sitting out here for hours on end. Wriggle those toes, flex those fingers. He pushed his neck even further down into the collar of his coat. It was an excellent position for observing the house; one he'd used before. He was fifty yards away from Alice's house with a clear view of her front door, and the darkness of the trawler's shadow meant he was invisible from the house, even from the road that passed between him and the house. On previous occasions, usually at dusk, he'd observed couples strolling along the lane just ten yards from where he sat and none ever noticed him. And this section of beach was nothing but a narrow shingle bank lined with these great smelly seaweed-striped hulks. No one walked along it.

The bag at his feet contained some jam sandwiches, a flask of coffee and, in a small lead tin, the two ounces of uranium pellets that he'd been keeping under their bed. His idea was to plant the tin in Alice's room. When found she would be implicated in the theft of nuclear materials and the whole affair would take on a very different light. The Authority would get involved and the police would suddenly have a motive on which to build a case against the dead girl. Perhaps Maynard discovered her and she killed him to stop him going to the police? Or they were in league with each other and one betrayed the other? It didn't really matter, as long as it deflected attention.

The knife was inside his breast pocket.

And Andrea was there with him. Not speaking but restless and agitated. He felt her in his fingertips and in his gut. He felt her crouching on his shoulders with talons.

Sunlight began to break through the bleary dawn, throwing a yellow wash on the little cottage where Alice slept.

Next came the mother. Overweight, red-faced, a bag slung over her shoulder. Frank seemed to remember Alice telling the dinner party that her mother worked as... what? He couldn't dredge up that detail.

So...just the brother to go. Then he could move, and get warm again.

• • •

When she heard the door shut behind Georgie she got up and went to the bathroom, had a pee and ran the bath. Now she was alone, thank God. In her family only her mother was talkative in the mornings, which often made breakfast-time tense. Her mother wanted to chat, everyone else wanted some peace and quiet, and they all started to grate on each other. Since Maynard's disappearance Alice had been even more grumpy than usual with her parents, but that was only to be expected, wasn't it?

She sat on the toilet for some time, her thoughts dissolving in the cloud of steam rising from the bath. She would speak to Parker today. Take the initiative. If it happened, she would tell her parents that she'd been offered this amazing opportunity, totally out of the blue, and although she didn't want to leave them, it really was too good to turn down…etcetera, etcetera. They wouldn't help her financially. Dad would be heartbroken to lose her (and she him), Mum wouldn't care less. So she would need to survive on her own. That was all right. She had some money saved up.

Typical. She'd let the hot tap run on too long. She squeezed it off and turned on the cold tap. Undressed.

• • •

Frank crossed the road, went up the alleyway at the side of the cottage and let himself into the back garden. It was a jumble of shrubs, pebbles and pieces of driftwood and he was careful to step only where his feet would make no sound. The bathroom window above him was an inch ajar, and steam was floating out.

Gambling that the noise of the running water would obscure what he was doing, he leant against the back door and tried the handle. Locked. But it was a flimsy door. He put his knee underneath the lock, crouched a little, drew back and then slammed forward. The wood around the lock splintered but didn't give. Quickly he stood back, gripped the door frame and kicked the door with the sole of his foot. Now it shattered and the door swung open. He hesitated on the threshold, listening for a reaction from inside the house. None came.

Through the kitchen, where the breakfast things were still out on the table, duck through the low doorway and into the hallway, where a big grandfather clock stood, incongruous and silent. At the foot of the stairs he hesitated again. Sickness swelled in him, his knees felt paper-thin, unable to support his weight.

Up you go, my boy, she whispered, *and get that blade out.*

He did as he was told, and yet there was just a glimmer of disobedience in his mind, like a faint signal being picked up from deep inner space. Up the stairs, creaking with every footfall, turning the knife handle in his palm. There were no taps running now but there was the low babble of a radio coming from a bedroom. On the landing he was faced with four closed doors.

Don't hesitate, just do it.

He wanted to go blundering into the wrong room, to give her a chance to get out of the bath and react – just a chance. But Andrea knew his thoughts, she knew his weaknesses. If he let the girl go…well, she would open up his scar again, and would keep slicing all the way down. He had no choice but to obey her.

You know which door it is.

He did. The handle was warm to the touch. The door swung open and he stepped inside. The bath was empty. He swivelled on his heel and saw her on the landing. She had a towel wrapped around her, bare white shoulders and shins, hair hanging in shining wet ribbons. She was dripping on the floorboards. In her hand there was a knife. Her expression was hard to judge.

Andrea came flying into his head with a terrible whistling sound and black malice, and he took a step forward, but they both knew he couldn't do it. Enough remained of his mind that he was moved by the sight of her youthfulness and vulnerability. She was just a girl, and he had no argument with her.

'You think you're protecting me,' she said in a faltering voice, 'but you're just like all the rest.'

'I was protecting you, I was,' he said, but even as he said it the words sounded hollow. He no longer understood what was happening to him.

You're weak.

'Yes, I am,' he said to Andrea. Alice frowned and took a step backwards towards the stairs.

Frank sank to his knees, dropped the knife and looked up at her.

'You think you're different but you're just like all the rest. Just a man. A pathetic man.'

Anger spread through him like fire, sparks flying to his synapses. Bitch! He was not just another man. He was not!

He grabbed the knife from the floor and lunged at her. She didn't give any ground and he saw her own blade, much bigger than his own, swiping through the air. The next moment was a slow-motion dance, silver flashing in the darkness, no pain, just the dull clunk of his knife on the floor and the twist of his body as he lost his balance. And as he lay at her feet he saw the droplets of water on her neck, the smoothness of her skin, the water spraying from her hair onto his face as she brought the knife down into his belly.

And he thought, she's so calm.

EPILOGUE

The boy gazed out of the car window, his eyes flickering across brown hills draped in low cloud. He remembered this long journey. Mummy said they came every year for Daddy's birthday. But he had never met his daddy because Daddy flew up to heaven while he was still cooking inside Mummy's tummy. And if Daddy was up in heaven why did they have to drive along the motorway for so long? It was all very confusing.

He felt Mummy's energy growing as they drove along smaller roads. When she had butterflies in her tummy she fidgeted; that was one of their secrets. Now she played with her hair, and pushed mysterious buttons inside the car. Now and then she glanced over her shoulder and gave him a tight smile. Nearly there. Good boy.

No more houses now. Just sheep and grass and sky. Then the big fence. This was something he remembered from last time. So high, with its bright yellow signs that he couldn't read but didn't need to. Danger, they said.

The car came to a stop. Mummy turned the radio off. In front of them were thick metal gates, more yellow signs. From a little hut a soldier walked towards the car and Mummy rolled down her window.

'Gail Banner,' she said. It always sounded funny to hear her other name.

The soldier looked at a sheet of paper in his hand and nodded. Then he bent down and peered in.

'And James, right?' he said, adding a wink. Winking was something the boy had been trying to achieve for ages and for this soldier to do it so easily annoyed him.

'Jimmy,' he said quickly and looked straight ahead with his determined face on. The soldier laughed, which annoyed Jimmy even more.

The gates opened and Mummy drove slowly through. This was a strange cold place. A grey building with no windows, lots more fences, big stone boxes. As they walked across the car park he was glad that Mummy held his hand snug. The wind growled in his ears. There was no one else around but Jimmy had the feeling they were being watched.

At the door to the grey building Mummy had to push a button then say her name. Then the door opened without anyone being on the other side. Ahead was a long straight corridor. Jimmy had never known anywhere so quiet. Only their footsteps and the tinkle of Mummy's jewellery. Afraid, he squeezed her hand and she winced. Ouch, not so hard, she was thinking.

At the end of the corridor was another door. Mummy led him through it and they came to a place he remembered, though whether he remembered it from real life or from dreams he couldn't tell. It was a big flat field of grass, criss-crossed with stone paths. Around it was a high stone wall with spiky wire on top. Embedded in the grass, if you looked, were metal squares with writing on. Names and dates, Mummy said. Every one of them was in heaven, but a piece of them was buried here. Deep in the earth, deeper than you can imagine. Encased in special boxes that would keep everyone safe for a thousand years. Jimmy didn't really understand this bit. It seemed like it might be connected to the doctors who ran tests on him every so often, pricking his finger to take blood and making him breathe into glass bottles.

Mummy led him along the paths to Daddy's square. It looked like all the rest but she stared at it for a long time, then knelt to wipe it with a tissue from her handbag. Together they'd chosen a set of colourful handkerchiefs for Daddy's birthday present. Mummy gave it to Jimmy and he placed it neatly on the metal square. Then Mummy produced one of Jimmy's best drawings (of a dragon in space) and tucked it underneath the handkerchiefs. Mummy cried a bit then gave Jimmy a cuddle. Her tears got his face wet.

'I miss your daddy. He was a fool but I loved him. A bloody fool. I could have saved him. If only he'd talked to me I could have saved him.'

This was beginning to get boring. Jimmy pulled at her hand and eventually she came with him. They left the field a different way, through a gate he hadn't seen before. Just beyond, there was a room where three soldiers stood talking in front of a row of flashing machines. The air smelled of soap and smoke.

'Long way to come,' said the first in a friendly voice.

'Sign here,' said the second, pushing a book and pen into Mummy's hands.

'You'll leave with a glow though eh,' said the third with a nasty smile. The other soldiers gave him angry looks, as if he'd said something very rude, and the soldier dipped his head to say he was sorry for that.

Then he crouched in front of Jimmy, smiling that smile that Jimmy was used to getting from grown-ups.

'Well anyway,' said the soldier. 'You're a special little lad aren't you?'

'Yes I am,' said Jimmy, which made the soldier chuckle.

'And I bet you look after your mum. How old are you, son?'

'Five,' said Jimmy. The soldier's breath was hot and stinky.

'And do you know how to shake hands, like a big man?'

The soldier held out his brown, crinkly hand and Jimmy held it as he'd been taught by his grandfather. The soldier squeezed a bit, so Jimmy adjusted his fingers to better grip three of the soldier's fingers, then squeezed back.

'Oh, and you're strong!' laughed the soldier.

Jimmy went on squeezing and soon enough the soldier's smile changed to a different expression. His eyes widened. Jimmy knew there were hard bits inside the fingers that he could snap if he wanted to. Bones, weren't they called? The soldier looked scared. His fellow soldiers were laughing at him. He deserved it.

'Ouch, that really hurts,' said the soldier.

When Jimmy let go the soldier had to wiggle his broken

fingers to get them working again. He was smiling but Jimmy could tell that was just pretend. I will look after my mummy, thought Jimmy, and he gazed up at her.

'I am strong,' he said, and couldn't help but giggle.

THE END

ABOUT THE AUTHOR

Paul Maunder is an author and journalist.

His 2018 memoir *The Wind at my Back* explores the connections between landscape, creativity and the writing process.

He was awarded a Faber bursary for his fiction and has an MA in Creative Writing from Royal Holloway, where he studied with the Poet Laureate, Andrew Motion.

He regularly publishes features and fiction in cycling magazines *Peloton* and *Rouleur*.

He lives in South London with his wife and two children.

If you have enjoyed *The Atomics*, do please help us spread the word – by posting a review on Amazon (you don't need to have bought the book there) or Goodreads; by posting something on social media; or in the old-fashioned way by simply telling your friends or family about it.

Book publishing is a very competitive business these days, in a saturated market, and small independent publishers such as ourselves are often crowded out by the big houses. Support from readers like you can make all the difference to a book's success.

Many thanks.

Dan Hiscocks
Publisher
Lightning Books